W9-CRV-054

TERROR
IN THE
SKY

AN
AMERICAN ADVENTURE
SERIES

TERROR
IN THE
SKY
LEE RODDY

Lyons Public Library
448 Cedar St.
P.O. Box 100
Lyons, OR 97358

DISCARD

BETHANY HOUSE PUBLISHERS
MINNEAPOLIS, MINNESOTA 55438

Copyright © 1991
Lee Roddy
All Rights Reserved

Published by Bethany House Publishers
A Ministry of Bethany Fellowship, Inc.
6820 Auto Club Road, Minneapolis, Minnesota 55438

Printed in the United States of America

Library of Congress Cataloging-in-Publication Data

Roddy, Lee, 1921–
    Terror in the Sky / Lee Roddy.
        p.   cm. — (An American adventure ; bk. 6)

    Summary: Struggling with school and a lack of money during the Depression, seventh grader Hildy is overwhelmed when the little girl she cares for after school is kidnapped, but God steps in in a remarkable manner.
    [1. Adventure and adventurers—Fiction.
2. Depression—1929—Fiction. 3. Christian life—Fiction.]
I. Title. II. Series: Roddy, Lee, 1921–   American adventure ; bk. 6.
PZ7.R6Te   1991
[Fic.]—dc20   91–11898
ISBN 1–55661–096–3   CIP
                                               AC

Virginia A. ("Slugger") Daniels
my very special friend,
with thanks for your
friendship, love, and prayers

LEE RODDY is a bestselling author and motivational speaker. Many of his more than 50 books, such as *Grizzly Adams*, *Jesus*, *The Lincoln Conspiracy*, the *D. J. Dillon Adventure Series*, and the *Ladd Family Adventures* have been bestsellers, television programs, book club selections or have received special recognition. All of his books support traditional moral, spiritual, and family values.

Contents

STRANGER AT THE RIVER

Sunday Afternoon

Cautiously, Hildy Corrigan took another step on silent bare feet. Her slender body tensed as her blue eyes strained to see ahead. She gingerly removed a long, wild blackberry vine that snagged on her homemade green dress. She peered across the four-foot-high tangle of vines in the remote river bottom.

"Listen!" she whispered, reaching back to clutch her cousin's arm. "There it is again! Hear it?"

Ruby Konning, also barefooted but wearing a boy's overalls and old shirt, trailed a half step behind. She whispered back, "I jist hear that thar ol' river." She had been in California only a few months and still spoke with an accent from her native Ozark Mountains.

"Shh!" Hildy hissed. "It's coming from across the river!" She also was a California newcomer but had lost her accent before coming west.

Hildy gazed across the hundred-yard-wide stream. The water was so shallow that she could clearly see stones on the bottom. On the far shore, a gravel bar ran along in front of a chalk-like bluff twenty feet high above the water. Hildy smelled the fragrance of cottonwoods and willows growing on this side of the river in the warm September afternoon.

"Maybe it's a haint!" Ruby said in a frightened whisper.

Hildy gave an impatient toss of her long brunette braids. She replied softly, "I keep telling you there's no such things as haunts!"

"Jist the same," her year-older cousin answered uneasily, "let's go someplace we know! If'n we got lost in here, nobody'd ever find us!" She anxiously turned to start the long trek back to the graveled county road.

"Look!" Hildy again pointed across the river. "The willows are moving! Duck down!"

"Why? We ain't doin' nothin' . . ."

Hildy broke off Ruby's sentence by suddenly reaching out, grabbing her cousin's wrist, and pulling her down behind a large cottonwood log.

The girls were best friends as well as cousins, so Ruby reluctantly crouched with Hildy in the shelter of the tree trunk.

They had gone exploring Lone River to see if any salmon had started upstream to spawn. Hildy and Ruby had pushed through dense brush and accidentally stumbled on this remote, unfamiliar spot.

In a moment Ruby let out a small sigh of relief. "It ain't nothin' but an ol' dawg!"

The biggest dog Hildy had ever seen trotted out of the willows on the opposite shore, about twenty feet to the right of the small bluffs. He was a mastiff of tawny brindle color with dark streaks like a tiger's stripes. The dog left the hardy Bermuda grass and walked onto a gravel bar to drink at the river's edge.

"Shore hope he's friendly-like," Ruby whispered.

"Shh!" Hildy interrupted. "Somebody's with him!"

A stoutly built man in his mid-thirties peered cautiously out of some willows. He wore high-top boots, tattered striped overalls, and a sweat-stained slouch hat. After a moment of furtive watching, the stranger stepped into the open carrying a galvanized bucket in each hand. He crunched across the gravel, set one bucket down, and threw the other's contents in a sweeping motion across the water.

"What's he a-doin'?" Ruby whispered. "Looks like he's throwin' away plain old dirt."

The stranger threw the contents of the second bucket over the water just as the dog looked up from his drinking. He barked sharply, looking directly at the hidden girls.

"He's done seen us!" Ruby exclaimed.

The man shaded his eyes with his free hand to stare across the river against the afternoon sun. "Hey!" he yelled in a rough voice. He dropped the empty bucket on the gravel bar with a clatter. "Why're you kids sneakin' around here?"

Hildy stood up from behind the log and raised her voice to be heard above the river's sounds. "We're not sneaking! We're . . ."

The man turned to the dog. "Sic 'em, Tige!" He swung his right arm in a sweeping command. "Go get 'em!"

The dog leaped into the shallow water.

Ruby cried, "I don't aim to let no dawg chaw on me! Feet, git me outta here!" She turned and ran.

Hildy hesitated as the stranger hurried along the gravel bar for a few steps. Then he waded quickly into the river behind the dog.

Hildy hated to run, but she sensed this was no time to stop and try reasoning with the pursuers. In one quick motion, she grabbed up the hem of her dress and jerked it above her knees so she could run faster. Barefooted, she raced after her cousin.

When Hildy drew abreast of Ruby, they pounded side by side through summer-dried weeds and under the huge valley oaks that grew inland on the river bottom. Wild grapevines trailed from some tree branches.

Hildy's eyes desperately searched ahead as she tried to remember how they'd gotten down to this unfamiliar area of densely overgrown river bottom. There were no people anywhere in sight. The only house was a good half mile away, perched grandly on top of the cliff overlooking the river.

Hildy felt a surge of hope when she recognized the Victorian mansion owned by Matthew Farnham. He also owned the bank in Lone River, the small rural town at the eastern end of California's great San Joaquin Valley. Hildy worked part-time for the Farnhams, caring for their two small children.

When Hildy glanced back, her hope died. The dog bounded over brush and stumps with powerful leaps. He was barking thunderously and gaining fast. Hildy's skin crawled with fear.

"He'll be on us in a minute!" she panted, almost feeling the dog's teeth closing on her bare legs. "Grab that next wild grape-vine and climb up into the tree!"

"Then that man'll git us!"

"Better him than the dog!"

Both girls looked up for trailing vines just as the man called sharply, "Yo, Tige! That's enough! Let 'em go!"

Hildy glanced back as the huge animal slid to a stop.

The man was slumped over, hands on his knees, obviously winded, but he raised his voice to shout at the girls. "If I ever see you two around here again, I'll let ol' Tige eat you alive! Now, get out of here!"

When the breathless girls had found their way to the un-paved country road, Hildy turned for a final look back. Shadows had started to fill the river bottom as sunset slipped closer. There was no sign of dog or man.

"Ruby, why d'you suppose he threw those buckets of dirt into the river instead of on the ground?"

"Who knows? I'm jist almighty glad that ol' dawg didn't ketch us!"

"That man sure was secretive. The way he acted, you'd think we'd stumbled onto his secret gold mine. But there's never been any gold down in this valley."

"Shore ain't none here now! Ain't nothin' much down here 'cepting this ol' Depression." The country was still deep in the economic disaster that had started five years ago in 1929.

Hildy started walking along the deserted country road. "You know," she mused, "if school weren't starting tomorrow, we could go back down there and check it out."

"You plumb crazy? Ye heerd what he said! Y'all better jist

think about gittin' ready fer school."

"Guess so," Hildy agreed. "But as soon as possible, I'm going back down there!"

The girls walked on the dirt shoulder of the road. Gravel hurt their bare feet too much to walk on the road itself.

Ruby asked, "Ye skeered to start school?"

"No. Fact is, I'm anxious. I want to win that hundred-dollar scholarship the Studebaker dealer's offering."

"Yeah! A hunnert dollars is a right smart lot of money, 'specially fer a seventh grader."

"I'll say! My daddy rides horseback sixteen hours a day, Monday through Saturday, to earn fifteen dollars. It takes him nearly seven weeks to make a hundred dollars. That's not enough to help me with college, so I've got to save every penny I can get. Winning that scholarship would help a lot!"

Ruby made an unladylike snorting noise. "Ye beat all I ever heard tell of! Wantin' a 'forever' home so bad yo're bound and determined to git a college eddy-cation! Why, we don't know ary a one who's ever gone to college!"

"I'm going," Hildy said firmly.

"But to win that hunnert dollars, ye got to write an essay!" She said the word as though it was an unspeakable thing.

Hildy nodded. "Plus be judged on citizenship and scholarship. But my whole future depends on winning, so I can become a teacher!" She took a deep breath and added, "Then I'll buy a 'forever' home where our family won't ever have to move again!"

Ruby said softly, "Ye shore got a powerful big dream fer somebody like you! I mean, bein' born in a sharecropper's cabin and then sort of goin' downhill from there. How many places you lived, anyhow?"

"I don't remember. Daddy moved so much, trying to get work. Let's see, in twelve years, I've lived in Arkansas, Missouri, Oklahoma, Texas, and Illinois."

Hildy glanced down at her knees, remembering that she still bore scars from when she'd picked cotton at age seven. After that, she'd done all kinds of work to earn a few pennies, including being a hired girl, mostly taking care of other people's kids. Hildy's family had been in California only three months, but she loved Lone River more than any place she'd ever been.

"The only way to stay here and get our 'forever' home," Hildy said quietly, "is to save every penny. Oh, don't you see, Ruby? I've got to win that scholarship!"

When the girls reached the barn-house where Hildy lived with her family, her uncle, Nate Konning, was waiting in his old borrowed Model T car to take his daughter to the ranch where they lived. The cousins didn't mention their experience at the river bottom.

That night, sleeping outside the barn-house in a shelter made of gunny sacks, Hildy dreamed that the big brindled dog had caught up with her at the river.

"No!" Hildy cried out in her sleep, thrashing about on a pallet of old quilts and coats, because the family couldn't afford a bed or even a cot.

She awoke with a start, her heart pounding. Her long, un-combed hair fell in a tangled mass across her face. Through the hair, she saw her pet raccoon nuzzling her chin while making chirring sounds.

Hildy shoved the hair out of her eyes and sat up in the old nightgown she'd sewn from flour sacks. "You want breakfast, Mischief?"

The girl crawled through the flaps of her makeshift room and hoisted the masked little animal to her favorite perch on the back of her owner's neck. "Brr!" Hildy said, glancing at the sky. "Yesterday it was in the eighties, but I can sure feel autumn coming this morning!"

The Corrigan family lived in the country, so there were no near neighbors to see Hildy as she hurried across the dusty barnyard in her nightgown. The raccoon held on to Hildy's tan-gled long hair with tiny, human-like front paws. The hind legs hung down on either side of the girl's neck.

Hildy lightly stroked the long ringtail dangling beside her right cheek. "Mischief, I wish they'd let me take you to school, but . . ."

She broke off her sentence at the sound of multiple motors.

She automatically looked down the long dusty driveway toward the Lombardy poplars beside the unpaved county road. There were no cars in sight.

Hildy frowned, turning in all directions, trying to locate the sound. Then a great long shadow passed the barn and fell on her. She looked up to the sky, her mouth falling open in surprise.

A huge sausage-shaped airship about the length of two football fields glided overhead. Hildy couldn't see the motors, but did see propellers rotating in silver flashes on the outside of the strange craft. The motors made a sound totally unlike any Hildy had ever heard.

She shaded her eyes against the sky's glare as the immense craft slid into full view from behind the barn's sheltering roof. Hildy saw the American insignia of a white star with a red circle in the middle against a round blue background. That was between the tail and the word *Navy* written on the side.

Hildy heard the barn door slide open fast. Her four younger towheaded sisters rushed outside. They were trailed by their stepmother, Molly. She was still in her nightgown, holding sixteen-month-old Joey on her right hip. Everyone looked up at the incredible sight.

"What *is* it?" ten-year-old Elizabeth asked in awe.

Hildy studied the giant rigid-frame airship as it slowly continued in an easterly direction. "I've never seen one, but it has to be a dirigible!"

"What's a dur-guh-bull?" seven-year-old Elizabeth asked.

"Di-ri-gi-ble," her stepmother replied, pronouncing the syllables. "Hildy's right! That's what is! Sometimes called a zeppelin. This's the first one I've ever seen, although I've seen pictures. Some are stationed at Sunnyvale, near San Francisco, about half a day's drive from here."

Elizabeth, always practical, protested, "But it's got no wings! How can it fly?"

Molly explained, "From what I've read, it's by gas held inside the long balloon part. That gas is called helium, which won't blow up or catch fire. But other countries, like Germany, use hydrogen, which is very dangerous. Dirigibles can be controlled and directed like an airplane. The crew is inside that little cabin with the windows, underneath the long part, near the front end."

Three-year-old Iola suddenly clutched Hildy's leg and buried her face in her older sister's nightgown. "I'm scared!" Iola said in a muffled voice.

Hildy bent and pulled the little girl into her arms. "It's nothing to be scared—"

"Car coming!" Elizabeth interrupted.

Everyone turned toward the Lombardy poplars at the end of the dusty lane. Hildy recognized her father's long Rickenbacker turning off the county road.

Hildy's younger sisters started yelling happily at the sight of their cowboy father, but Hildy's heart plunged sickeningly. She turned to her stepmother, whose face reflected Hildy's sudden concern.

Hildy exclaimed, "Something's wrong, or he wouldn't be home so early in the morning!"

Chapter Two

TROUBLE EVERYWHERE

Monday Morning

The dirigible was forgotten when everyone saw Joe Corrigan driving up. He always left the barn-house before dawn to begin his day riding as a cowboy for the nearby Woods Brothers Ranches. He seldom returned before dusk, so his arriving in the morning was a bad sign.

An anguished thought struck Hildy. *Oh, I hope he didn't lose his job! Then we'd have to move! I don't want to do that ever again!*

Hildy lifted Mischief down from her perch on the back of her neck. The raccoon protested noisily as Hildy set her on the ground. Still in her nightgown, Hildy began running toward the approaching car. Her sisters and stepmother followed.

The long, black Rickenbacker skidded to a stop in a cloud of dust. Hildy jumped up on the running board of the straight-eight sedan. Her father couldn't afford to buy this old car, so he'd traded his mechanical services for it. Then he'd converted it to burn cheap stove oil instead of expensive gasoline.

Hildy stuck her head inside the driver's open window. "Daddy! What's wrong?"

Joe Corrigan tipped his sweaty cowboy hat back with a strong forefinger. His face was darkly tanned, but his forehead was white where the hat had been moved from its usual position. He managed a weak smile and reached out to tenderly touch each of the children. "The ranch truck broke down, so the foreman sent me in to town to get parts to repair it. I took an extra minute to run out and tell you what else he said."

Hildy sensed it hadn't been something good.

Her father continued, "He says times are so hard he has to let some riders go."

Molly whispered in sudden fear, "Not you, Joe?"

"Don't know yet. The foreman just said he was letting us know a few days early in case one of us riders had another job lined up. Nobody does."

Hildy tried to sound confident in front of her little sisters. "He'll keep you on, Daddy! You're the best rider he's got!"

Joe Corrigan reached out and lightly stroked Hildy's uncombed hair. He smiled at her, then abruptly changed the subject. "You going to work for the Farnhams after school today?"

Hildy nodded. "Got to save for college," she said. "Besides, I love taking care of Connie and Dickie."

"You be careful, Hildy." He patted her cheek with a strong, calloused hand. "Don't let them wander off. They're so close to the river they could be in it before you know it."

"I'll be careful."

"I know you will. Now, you'd better get ready for school, and I've got to get back to the ranch."

An hour later, dressed in her plain blue dress and new brown shoes, Hildy walked down the lane to wait for the school bus. She carried her shiny lunch pail, which once had contained lard. Her little sisters attended a different school, so their bus wouldn't come until later.

Hildy silently prayed that her father wouldn't lose his job, because that would surely mean the family would have to move again, maybe away from Lone River.

When the ancient red school bus stopped, the door swung open, and Hildy stepped up quickly. She smiled at the driver. He had straw-colored hair parted in the middle and slicked back on both sides. He ignored Hildy and scowled into the large mirror above his steering wheel.

The seventh and eighth graders already on the Northside Grammar School bus momentarily stopped their noise to look at Hildy.

Hildy glanced around for Ruby and saw her sitting alone four seats back on the opposite side of the bus from where Hildy had entered. She started toward Ruby, smiling in greeting.

Ruby's short blonde hair was neatly combed. She wore a plain white dress that fell halfway between her knees and new black shoes. Her lips were set in a grim line, and her hazel eyes burned with inner emotion.

Suddenly concerned for her cousin, Hildy started to move toward the empty seat just as the other kids turned their attention from Hildy to Ruby.

A big girl with short black hair mimicked Ruby's accent, but with great exaggeration. "Would you-all say that ag'in—in English?"

As the others roared with laughter, Ruby let out a screech. "I'll snatch ye baldheaded!" she cried, standing up and reaching toward the tormentor's hair.

The bus driver yelled, "You! New girl! Sit down! Zelpha and the rest of you—leave her alone!"

Hildy slid into the seat beside Ruby as the girl the driver had called Zelpha turned to whisper something to her seatmate. They both laughed.

Hildy glanced nervously around. "What's going on?"

Ruby muttered darkly, "I was jist a-tryin' to be friendly like, howdyin' to ever'body, ye know, when that big gal commenced a-pickin' on me!"

"Forget her!" Hildy replied, lowering her voice and leaning close to her cousin. "Daddy might lose his job."

Ruby's face changed from anger to concern. "No!"

Hildy quickly explained.

Ruby shrugged. "At least he's workin' full time. Muh pore ol' daddy's still jist a-pickin' up odd jobs now an' then—'sides his preachin' when he kin, but that don't never pay much."

The bus rumbled toward town while the cousins discussed

the possibility that both their fathers might move. If Hildy's father lost his cowboy job, he certainly would move. Ruby's father was trying to make up his mind about accepting a call to a church in the Ozarks. Neither girl wanted their fathers to move, because the cousins were too good friends to be willingly parted.

The girls finally exhausted their speculation about whether or not they'd have to move. Hildy changed the subject. "I dreamed about that stranger we saw down at the river, and his dog caught me."

"Lucky it was jist a dream."

"I know, but I wish . . ." she let her voice trail off.

"Ye wish Spud was here, huh?" Ruby guessed. "Him and his dog, Lindy, so's they could go with you back down to that river, 'cause I got too many smarts to go ag'in!"

The mention of Spud made Hildy feel strange. She and Ruby had met him three months ago when they were in the Ozarks. Hildy and Spud had become good friends but Ruby often resented the boy, so they didn't always get along.

"Wonder how he's doing?" Hildy mused.

Ruby didn't like Spud. She said with some feeling, "I shore hope he's back in Brooklyn with his family, and he won't never bother us ag'in!"

Hildy sometimes secretly wished she hadn't urged Spud to return home and try making up with his drunken father. That was a few weeks ago, and Hildy hadn't heard a word from the boy.

"But," Hildy admitted, glancing at her cousin, "if Spud were here, I'm sure he and Lindy would go to the river with me. Maybe we could figure out why that man acted so strangely, and why he threw dirt in the river instead of just dumping it on the ground."

"Fergit Spud!" Ruby snapped. "We ain't never a-gonna see him ag'in, and I say that's good riddance!"

The cousins fell silent when the bus turned onto the downtown Lone River street that took them past their new school. It was a large, aging, two-story, red-brick building squatting massively on the southeast corner of a square block. Steep stairs led up to the second floor.

The school ground was bare dirt pounded to fine dust by countless seventh and eighth graders. On the far end of the playground two long, low, wooden bus sheds stood in need of repair and paint.

When the bus stopped at the first shed, Hildy and Ruby let all the other students disembark first. Hildy watched the one called Zelpha, hoping she was finished picking on Ruby.

As the cousins rounded the bus shed, each carrying their round lunch pails, Hildy saw Zelpha greeting two other girls who'd obviously been waiting for her. The one called Tessie had mouse-colored hair worn in bangs. She was taller than either Hildy or Ruby. The other girl, Edna, was shorter. She had auburn hair and more freckles than a turkey egg.

Hildy heard Zelpha speak in a stage whisper meant to be heard. "We'd better walk upwind from those two."

Ruby let out a strangled sound of anger, but Hildy gripped her cousin's arm to hold her back. "Ignore them!"

The freckled girl asked sarcastically, "Okies, huh?"

Ruby jerked away from Hildy's restraining hand and shouted at the three girls. "We're not Okies!"

"Doesn't matter where you're from," the dark-haired Zelpha explained grandly with a toss of her head. "Okies, Arkies, poor white trash—you've both got that look, and we don't like it! Isn't that right?"

Her two companions nodded vigorously, grinning in a tormenting way at the cousins.

Ruby's short temper erupted. "Why, ye bunch of whangdoodle flatlanders! There'll never come a day in yore lives when any of you's as good as either of us!"

"Easy, Ruby!" Hildy cautioned, again reaching out and gripping her cousin's hand. Hildy forced a friendly smile. "I'm Hildy Corrigan, and this is my cousin, Ruby Konning."

Zelpha said haughtily, "We don't care who you are!"

"No, we don't!" Tessie, the girl with mouse-colored hair sneered. "Why don't you both go back where you. . . ?"

She didn't get to finish. Ruby dropped her lunch pail on the ground. Her arms, firm and fast as a boy's from a lifetime of tomboy roughhousing, struck with the speed of a rattlesnake. With her right hand, she gripped Zelpha's bobbed black hair. With the other hand she grabbed for Tessie's bangs.

Tessie was too fast, jerking her head back out of the way. But Zelpha let out a startled yell as Ruby began spinning her in a dusty circle by the hair.

Ruby gritted through clenched teeth, "Y'all take that back! An' say 'uncle' real quick if'n ye don't want to git scalped the hard way!"

"Ruby, please!" Hildy cried. "Don't. . . !"

She broke off her words as Edna reached out suddenly, grabbing for Hildy's right braid. At the same instant, Tessie reached for Hildy's left braid. With cries of triumph, the two girls backed off. Each held a long braid, so Hildy was jerked both ways at once.

Edna exclaimed, "Make your friend let go of Zelpha, or me'n Tessie'll pull you apart!"

Other kids raced across the school yard and surrounded the five girls with shouts of "Fight! Fight!"

Hildy dropped her lunch pail and grabbed both braids close to her head to ease the pain, but Tessie and Edna kept yanking her around.

"Break it up! Break it up!" a man's voice commanded.

When the two girls let go of her braids, Hildy's head ached.

Ruby had let go of Zelpha's hair as the bus driver pushed through the crowd.

He glared at Hildy and Ruby, saying, "You again!"

Ruby protested, "They started it!"

"Did not!" Zelpha exclaimed, adjusting her hair. "These Okies started it, Mr. Henderson!"

Tessie and Edna confirmed the lie, causing Ruby to grab for them.

The bus driver stopped her. "I thought so!" he said grimly. "Zelpha, Edna, and Tessie, go to your class." He took Hildy and Ruby by their arms. "You two are going to see the principal!"

Hildy and Ruby reclaimed their lunch pails and tried to explain what had really happened. The bus driver wouldn't listen.

He steered them into the school building and down the hallway filled with noisy students to a wooden door with a frosted window. A sign read *Ebenezer Wiley, Principal.*

The driver opened the door, giving Hildy a whiff of mildew and age common to old buildings. There wasn't much money in 1934, the middle of the Depression. Schools received only the bare necessities.

A tiny wisp of a woman with glasses looked up from behind her desk. The bus driver nodded curtly in greeting. "Miss Perkins, I've got to see Mr. Wiley."

Without waiting for the secretary to reply, the driver shoved Hildy and Ruby through a second open door into an inner office. It was gloomy, with only a small dirty window and a long electric bulb for light hanging over a rolltop desk. A baldheaded man of medium build wearing a brown suit swiveled away from the desk in a squeaking chair.

"What's this, Mr. Henderson?" he demanded, lowering his chin and looking over the tops of gold wire-rimmed glasses.

"This blonde Okie—I mean, new girl from out of state started trouble on the bus, then continued it on the school grounds. After we got to school, both these girls started a fight with Zelpha Krutz and her two friends."

"Zelpha?" the principal asked, leaping to his feet.

"She's okay," the bus driver said. "I got there in time to stop it pretty fast."

Hildy wondered briefly why the principal had shown such sudden interest in the girl called Zelpha. He hadn't asked if Hildy or Ruby were hurt, although their clothes were dirty and rumpled. Hildy could feel a scratch on her right cheek.

The principal's voice was cold and hard. "New girls, hmm? What are your names?" He sat down again.

"I'm Hildy Corrigan. She's Ruby Konning. We're cousins."

Hildy started to tell what had really happened, but Mr. Wiley broke in. "Do you two realize who Zelpha Krutz is?"

Hildy and Ruby clutched their lunch pails and shook their heads.

"She's the daughter of Karl Krutz, president of the school board of trustees."

Hildy didn't know much about school boards, but the principal's words made her realize Mr. Krutz was someone special in Lone River. So was his daughter.

The principal said sternly, "You new girls must learn that we don't allow fighting here." He half-turned in the protesting chair and reached for a razor strop hanging on the wall beside his desk.

Hildy gulped at sight of what most kids incorrectly called a strap. Her grandfather Corrigan had one like it. The horsehide strap was pliable on one side for finishing. The other side was corrigated for sharpening razors. It had an oiled black finish, leather padded handle, and nickel-plated swivel to hang it up. Grandpa Corrigan used the strop to sharpen his straight razor, because he didn't like the "new" safety razors. But other men used the strop for a different reason.

Ruby let out a low moan. "Hildy," she whispered, "he's a-gonna whup us!"

Chapter Three

UNEXPECTED CLASSMATES

Monday Morning

Hildy couldn't believe what was happening. "Sir, it wasn't our fault!"

The principal lightly drew the razor strop across his open left palm. "That's what they all say! But the girl you two picked on is . . ."

Ruby interrupted, "Don't ye at least want to hear our side of it?"

Seeing the angry look the principal gave Ruby, Hildy decided Mr. Wiley wasn't going to listen to anything said against Zelpha. Hildy guessed that the principal owed his job to the school trustees. In these hard times, he wasn't going to anger the board president.

No teacher or principal had ever laid a hand on Hildy, but now she realized that was about to change. She hurt inside with the thought of being humiliated this way, especially because she wasn't guilty of anything deserving punishment.

The secretary stuck her head in the door. "Mr. Wiley, the janitor just called from the basement. Something about the furnace again. He wants you to see it right away."

The principal frowned, then nodded. "Be right there." He turned and replaced the strop on the hook.

Hildy and Ruby looked at each other and sighed with relief.

Mr. Wiley added, "You girls report back here to me right after school, and we'll finish where we left off."

Hildy exclaimed, "I can't stay after school! I've got to help Mrs. Farnham!"

The principal asked in a surprised tone, "You don't mean Beryl—that is, Mrs. Matthew Farnham?"

Hildy nodded vigorously, her long braids jerking emphatically. "I'm their hired girl—part-time, I mean."

"You are?" Mr. Wiley sounded doubtful.

Ruby blurted, "She shore is! Sometimes I also hire out to them, like pushin' Mrs. Farnham's wheelchair and doin' housework. Hildy takes care of their little kids."

"Dickie and Connie," Hildy added. "He's six. She's four."

The principal's voice softened. "I know." He studied the girls thoughtfully. He still seemed to doubt that the two girls knew Lone River's most influential family or worked part-time for them.

Hildy realized this and made a suggestion. "You could telephone Mrs. Farnham. She'll tell you herself."

The principal's eyes narrowed thoughtfully. "Yes," he said, "we could do that. Please step into Miss Perkins' office and use her phone."

The girls and bus driver followed the principal into the outer office. The secretary looked up from her desk.

The principal said with a sort of half-smile of doubt, "Hildy would like to use your phone."

Hildy felt a moment of panic because she had never made a phone call. She started to explain this as the instrument was handed to her, but a bell rang loudly in the hallway. Hildy waited until it had stopped.

There was nothing to do but confess her inexperience. Hildy said, "Uh—I don't know how to—use one of—these."

For a second the principal seemed to doubt this too. Then

he smiled as though confident he was calling Hildy's bluff. "Miss Perkins," he said, "get Matt Farnham's home at once."

"Yes, sir." She lifted the upright instrument.

Mr. Wiley turned to the bus driver who'd been standing silently in the doorway. "Mr. Henderson, you may return to your duties."

As the driver left, the principal studied Hildy, who was watching closely to see how a telephone worked. Miss Perkins removed the earpiece from its hook and settled it against her right ear. With her left hand, she jiggled the hook several times. Then she said into the raised mouthpiece, "Nellie? This is Principal Wiley's office. Put us through to Matthew Farnham's residence at once, please."

Hildy was aware that the principal now seemed to be eyeing her with less doubt.

Miss Perkins announced, "It's ringing." She handed the instrument to Hildy.

When Hildy hesitated, the principal reached out and took the earpiece in his right hand and the rest of the instrument in his left. "Hello? Farnham residence? Mrs. Farnham? Mr. Wiley here—Ebenezer Wiley, the principal. I have a couple of students in my office—Hildy Corrigan and Ruby Konning; who say— What? Yes, of course. I'll put her on at once!" He handed the instrument to Hildy, his face showing surprise.

Hildy gingerly took the two pieces of phone and tried to imitate what she'd seen the principal do. She spoke into the mouthpiece. "Hello?"

Mrs. Farnham's voice sounded tired. "Hildy? Is something wrong?"

"No, ma'm. The principal . . ." She stopped in midsentence as he waved both hands in front of her.

He whispered, "Don't tell her! Please!"

Hildy hesitated, thinking fast. "Uh—how're Connie and Dickie?"

"They're fine. Hildy, I thought you didn't know how to use the telephone."

Hildy thought fast. It wasn't in her nature to lie, but she also didn't want to get in any more trouble with the principal. She said, "You've taught me some, and—Mr. Wiley's sort of letting me practice with the school phone."

Hildy saw the principal sigh and seem to relax. She started to say goodbye, but Mrs. Farnham's voice stopped her. "Hildy, I'm glad you called. I need to see the doctor this afternoon. So could you come directly here after school instead of going to your home first and walking over later, as we planned?"

"You want me there right after school?" Hildy asked.

Instantly, the principal reached over and covered the mouth-piece with his hand. He whispered, "Tell her you'll be there!"

Hildy relayed the message, said goodbye, and handed the phone back to the secretary.

Mr. Wiley's attitude had totally changed from what it was when the cousins first entered his office. "Girls, I hope you'll both forgive Mr. Henderson for bringing you . . ." He stopped as a second bell rang loudly in the hallway.

When the ringing had stopped and the halls were quiet, he continued, "That was the tardy bell. Since this is the first day of school, and apparently nobody was injured in the little incident that brought you two to my office, let's just forget the whole thing, shall we?"

"Suits us, huh, Hildy?" Ruby said.

Hildy nodded, too relieved to speak.

The principal's voice was now very friendly. "I knew that the Farnhams, having both come from a hardship background, often employed children of . . . Well, no matter. Do you girls know where your homerooms are?"

Hildy and Ruby shook their heads. Hildy hadn't even heard about a homeroom.

Mr. Wiley asked, "What grade are you in?"

Hildy said, "We're both seventh."

"That'll be 7-B, Miss Krutz's class," he said.

"Miss Krutz?" Hildy asked anxiously.

"Poppy Krutz is a sister to Karl Krutz, president of the school board of trustees," Mr. Wiley explained. "Zelpha, the girl with whom you two . . . Well, Zelpha is Miss Krutz's niece."

The principal turned to the outer door. "Because the tardy bell has rung, Miss Krutz will not admit you without a slip from the office. However, I'll explain to her, and it'll be all right. Come on, please."

Miss Perkins reminded him, "The janitor's waiting in the basement."

"Let him wait," the principal replied. He smiled again at the cousins.

Ruby returned the smile, but Hildy didn't. Knowing that Zelpha Krutz, who'd caused all their troubles, was a niece to Miss Krutz, the homeroom teacher, gave Hildy a very uneasy feeling.

"One thing more," Mr. Wiley added, eyeing the girls' faces and clothing as he led them down the now quiet halls. "I trust you two are not going to be like most of your—I mean, the kind of out-of-staters who arrive here from the Dust Bowl, usually dirty and unwashed, then drift on."

Hildy glanced at her soiled hands and felt the smudges on her face. "Ruby and I were clean when we left home."

"I suppose you were," Mr. Wiley replied. "A stop at the girls' lavatory will get you tidied up. But it's a shame about your clothes. In these hard times . . ." He let his words trail off.

Hildy looked in dismay at the blue cotton dress her step-mother had made with needle and thread because they had no sewing machine. When she saw her shoes, Hildy groaned. They were supposed to last the whole school year, but they were already scuffed and dirty.

Moments later, the principal opened a classroom door with neat black letters: 7-B Homeroom. Hildy noticed that it was an outside room with huge windows on the far side. Leaves were turning brown on the row of sycamore trees at the edge of the school grounds. Under the bank of open windows, steam radiators ran the length of the room beside the row of desks. The other walls held portraits of Washington and Lincoln, the American flag, blackboards, and posters. There was a door at the back leading to the cloakroom.

The teacher stood behind her desk. She was about six feet

tall, Hildy guessed, and not much bigger around than one of her seventh-grade girls. Miss Krutz had graying brown hair parted in the middle and pulled back into a bun. She wore a plain black dress reaching to her ankles and matching shoes.

"Miss Krutz," the principal said as the entire roomful of pupils looked up at the late arrivals, "these new students—Hildy Corrigan and Ruby Konning—are assigned to your homeroom. Please excuse their tardiness. They were in my office—on important business."

Hildy heard a titter and glanced at the back of the room. Zelpha Krutz sat near the back in the row of desks next to the radiator. Two empty seats were directly in front of her. The freckled girl called Edna sat opposite Zelpha in the second row from the window. Tessie, the big girl with bangs, sat behind Edna.

Miss Krutz turned hard gray eyes on the two newcomers. She did not smile. "Thank you, Mr. Wiley. Girls, those will be your desks." She pointed. "Ruby, you take the first one. However, I suggest you first put your lunches in the cloakroom."

In the cloakroom, Hildy whispered, "Do you realize I'm going to be sitting directly in front of Zelpha?"

"Shore do! An' we'll both be acrost the aisle from them other two o'nry gals! I don't like that one little bit! An' I shore don't like havin' that Zelpha's aunt fer our teacher, neither!"

"We'll have to make the best of it!"

Ruby grumbled, "Well, they better leave me alone!"

When the cousins returned to the classroom, the principal had gone. Miss Krutz turned cold eyes on the cousins. "Naturally, I accept Mr. Wiley's apology for your tardiness," she said disapprovingly. "But I warn you never to do it again."

Ruby protested as she walked toward her desk, "It weren't our fault, nohow! It was—"

Miss Krutz interrupted sternly. "I am not interested in excuses! However, I am interested in the proper use of English, and in the appearance of my students."

Laughter from the other students died out at Miss Krutz's silent glare. She asked, "How old are you, Ruby?"

Ruby shifted uneasily. "Thirteen. Hildy's twelve."

"Does that mean you were held back a year?" The teacher's voice was crisp. When Ruby nodded, Miss Krutz nodded. "I assumed that from the colloquial accent."

Ruby replied with some warmth, "It's not co-low—what you said. I'm from the Ozark Mountains, an' proud of it! But Hildy, well, she's been thar an' jist about ever' place else."

All the students snickered until Miss Krutz picked up a ruler and tapped it sharply on the desk. "Silence!"

It fell like a cold blanket over the twenty-plus students while Hildy's face flushed at the unfairness of her cousin being humiliated in front of everyone. Hildy said, "It wasn't her fault she's a year behind."

"I do not care to discuss the matter now, Hildy!" the teacher said. "You two go down the hall and clean up, then return. Be prompt about it! You've already lost enough valuable time."

In the girls' lavatory, the cousins washed at basins mounted below large mirrors. Ruby fumed, "I'd like to git even with them three gals!"

"Now, Ruby! Don't talk like that. It'll only get us into more trouble, and I've got to win that scholarship."

Ruby flared, "Ye a-gonna blame me if'n ye don't git it on accounta the things that done happened today?"

Hildy was used to her cousin's sudden outbursts of anger. They rarely lasted long, so Hildy usually overlooked them. She said evenly, "I'm not blaming anybody. I just don't want any more trouble."

"Ye already got trouble up to yore eyeballs! That Zelpha an' her two friends done already set out to make life miserable fer both of us. And ye heard the principal say Zelpha's kin to both our teacher and the boss of the school trustees. Ye got no chance a-tall!"

"I don't believe that!"

"Yo're so dadblamed stubborn, Hildy! I kin see right now—this is gonna be a turr'ble year!"

CHAPTER FOUR

THE PRODIGAL
COMES—AND GOES

Monday

Hildy and Ruby took their seats while Miss Krutz continued her first-day orientation lecture. "As I was saying, every morning after first reporting here to your homeroom, you will move from class to class during each period. You'll have different teachers, but I can tell you what each will require in basic materials."

She picked up several items from her desk and held each up as she mentioned it. "You will each need a three-hole binder, protractor, compass, and penholders. No fountain pens, just one like this into which the point will be inserted."

She demonstrated, adding, "You'll need extra points because you'll break or lose some. These items are available at the five-and-dime store. You'll be using pen and ink for the first time, so your mothers will have to make pen wipers."

Hildy listened to instruction on how pieces of soft flannel were to be loosely bound and carried from class to class. Then the use of inkwells was explained. Every student had a small glass bottle of black ink nestled in a round hole at the top right-hand corner of each desk. A pen was dipped into the ink to write. Since ink took a long time to dry, a blotter was used to keep it from smearing on the paper. Any ink remaining on the pen point was to be wiped off on the flannel.

Miss Krutz turned to the blackboard and picked up a piece of chalk. She neatly printed the name Emery Stanway. Miss Krutz explained, "As you all must have read in the local weekly newspaper, Emery Stanway, our . . ."

Hildy didn't hear the rest. She felt a slight movement of her right braid. She unconsciously jerked her head, sending the braid sailing into the aisle before it flopped wetly against her bare arm. Hildy blinked in surprise and glanced down.

Black ink glistened freshly on her right forearm. Hildy's eyes sought the end of her braid. It was soaked with ink.

Tessie and Edna stifled giggles from across the aisle. The teacher whirled around, her sharp eyes probing for the cause of the disturbance.

"Hildy!" Miss Krutz snapped. "What are you doing?"

Hildy turned to look at the girl behind her, but Zelpha was innocently gazing out the window. "Uh . . ." Hildy began, understanding that Zelpha had dipped the braid in an inkwell. "It's all right," she said.

"Here!" Miss Krutz said, walking quickly down the aisle with an ink-stained cloth. "Clean yourself up. And the rest of you students—please learn to keep everything out of the inkwells except the pens."

As the teacher turned back toward the front of the room, Hildy heard Zelpha, Tessie, and Edna snickering. Hildy's face burned with embarrassment that her teacher seemed to think she was such a backwoods girl she didn't even know how to handle ink.

Ruby half-turned in her seat in front of Hildy and whispered, "Zelpha done that a-purpose, ye know!"

Hildy nodded but said nothing as Miss Krutz reached her desk and turned around. "As I was saying, all of you must have read about Emery Stanway, our local Studebaker dealer. Each year he offers a one-hundred-dollar scholarship to a student in the seventh grade.

"Each of you is eligible to enter, but I warn you: infractions of rules will quickly eliminate some of you. As you leave for your second class, please pick up a copy of the rules, which I'll leave on the corner of my desk."

As the bell rang for students to leave for second-period classes, Zelpha stayed behind to speak with her aunt. Hildy picked up a page of scholarship rules. Zelpha's two friends pushed close to Hildy and Ruby as they entered the bustling hallway.

Hildy glanced at the rules. "An essay on dirigibles . . ."

She was interrupted by Tessie's voice. "Are you two dumb enough to think you can win that money?"

Ruby shrugged, glaring at the big girl with bangs of mouse-colored hair. "Makes no never-mind to me," Ruby said, "but Hildy plans to win that hunnert dollars."

Tessie and Edna giggled.

"What's so funny?" Ruby demanded angrily.

Tessie asked, "You know who the judges are?"

Hildy and Ruby shook their heads, making the other three girls smirk.

Tessie explained, "There are three judges. Miss Krutz is one, mostly on deportment. In case you don't know, that means behavior."

"Yeah!" Edna added, "and Mr. Wiley's a judge on citizenship!"

Hildy asked, "Who's judging the essay?"

Tessie laughed. "Zelpha's father!"

"That ain't fair!" Ruby protested.

Hildy nodded, feeling that Zelpha should not be able to compete if her father is a judge. She fought against a sense of concern as she and Ruby started toward their next class, leaving the giggling friends behind.

Ruby asked gently, "Ye feelin' real bad?"

Hildy nodded, because the scholarship represented so much hope for her future. "It's hard to imagine how I could have gotten off to a worse start."

The cousins approached the large double glass doors that led outside. Hildy glanced through them and stopped in surprise. "There's Lindy!"

"Lindy?"

"Spud's dog!" With rising hope, Hildy looked around the seething mass of students in the crowded hallway. "Spud must be . . . There he is!" She pointed and waved, but the boy was looking the other way. "He's back!"

Hildy started pushing through the kids in front of her. "Go on, Ruby! I'll catch up with you in a minute."

"Don't be late!" her cousin warned, but Hildy barely heard. She hurried through the crowd to where Spud stood by the front door, neck stretched, green eyes searching.

As the crowds parted momentarily, Hildy saw that fourteen-year-old Spud wore a blue work shirt too big for his body, torn overalls, and what was left of oversized shoes. He still proudly wore an aviator cap in honor of his hero, Charles A. Lindbergh, the man who'd made aviation history by flying the Atlantic alone in a single-engine monoplane just seven years before.

Hildy was beside him before he saw her. "Looking for someone?" she asked breathlessly, her smile wide.

"Greetings and felicitations!" he said, grinning at her from a ruddy face sprinkled with freckles. He was several inches taller than Hildy. He had wide shoulders, a narrow waist, and hands too big for his body. He pushed his aviator cap back on his forehead with a freckled right hand, exposing reddish hair.

"You're back!" she exclaimed, delight in her voice. "Oh, Spud, I missed—I missed your fancy big words!" Then Hildy frowned and her tone changed to concern. "Didn't it work out when you went home?"

"Home?" There was a sharp, bitter edge to the boy's voice. "I don't have a home!"

"Oh, Spud!" Hildy's heart suddenly ached for her friend. "You went all the way to Brooklyn—"

"And all the way back," the boy broke in grimly. "When the prodigal son arrived at the family domicile after not communicating with anyone for two years, my mother was glad to see me. But my old man just grunted when he saw me. He soon got drunk—as usual—and kicked me out after giving me this."

He turned his head slightly and raised the left flap of his aviator cap where it hung down his cheek.

Hildy stifled a small cry at sight of a fading but still noticeable purple bruise at the jawline. "Oh, Spud!" she whispered. "It's all my fault! I talked you into going back even after what you'd told me before about how your home life had been. But I thought—"

The boy broke in sharply. "I didn't have to listen to you. It's not your fault. However, after seeing how you and your family get along, I wanted . . . well, I thought it was worth trying it again with my old man. But . . ." He shrugged and lapsed into silence.

"I don't know what to say."

"Only one thing to say, Hildy. That's why Lindy and I came back three thousand miles." His tone softened. "I came to say goodbye."

Hildy's heart plummeted like a stricken bird. She opened her mouth to protest, but Spud raised a big hand.

"You're the only person in my whole life—well, you and some others around here—who ever made me feel . . ." He stopped, shrugged and added, "Anyway, I wanted to say good-bye before I started hoboing for good."

The hallway had grown quiet but Hildy was not aware of it. "You can't go!" she protested. "I—I mean, people around here like you—a lot."

"When we met," the boy replied softly, "back there in the Ozarks last June, I was on my way to Chicago."

"I remember."

"Instead, I came on out here to Lone River. But now I'm going back to see the Windy City for myself."

A bell clanged with ominous finality, making Hildy jump. "Oh, that's the last bell! I'm tardy! Miss Krutz will count that against me! I've got to run, but please don't go until we've had a chance to talk some more. Meet me after school. Please?"

Spud hesitated, looking out the large glass door. "Lindy's ready to start for Chicago." He indicated the bobtailed Airedale named after Lindbergh.

"Please?" Hildy repeated, totally forgetting her commitment to go directly to the Farnhams. "Meet me by the bus sheds!" She turned and dashed down the hallway without waiting for an answer.

She rounded a corner at a dead run and almost collided with Miss Krutz. "So!" the teacher said frostily. "You're also late for your second class, I see." She looked down from her great height. "Is this the way you expect to compete for the Studebaker award?"

Hildy started to explain, but Miss Krutz spoke first. "After all your other classes are over, I shall expect you to return to homeroom and stay after school."

"Stay after. . . ?" Hildy's voice cracked, knowing Spud would be waiting for her. "Miss Krutz, I can't!"

"Don't tell me what you can't do, young lady! Be in my room promptly! Then you and I shall have a talk!"

The rest of the morning was a time of anguish for Hildy. She was deeply concerned for Spud and for herself, but she was unable to share her emotions with Ruby until the noon hour.

They entered the crowded cloakroom together to get their lunch pails. Ruby reached up to the shelf above the coat hooks. She asked, "What happened to you between first and second period?"

"Tell you outside," Hildy said, glancing around at the other students.

As the cousins skipped down the steep stairs and onto the school grounds, Hildy looked around for a place to talk privately. She led the way past students sitting on benches that stretched the length of the red-brick building's west wall. Hildy and Ruby dodged sharp thorns of pyracantha bushes growing beside the back end of the school.

Ruby pointed ahead. "Wouldja lookee thar? Must be whar all the teachers park their cars. Most ever' single one of them's a Studebaker. Now I know why that Mr. Stanway gives away that hunnert dollars."

Hildy was only mildly interested, but glanced at the line of cars. In a year when almost nobody had a new one, Hildy judged three were this year's model Studebaker. Except for a Hudson, a Chevrolet, and an ancient Essex, all the older cars had the distinctive sweeping *S* logo on the red background that marked them as Studebakers.

"I have to tell you about Spud," Hildy said, finding an unoccupied bench. She repeated her conversation with Spud and the unfortunate encounter with Miss Krutz afterward. Hildy concluded, "So would you meet him after school and ask him to wait for me? I'll be along as soon as Miss Krutz lets me go."

Ruby's hazel eyes opened wide. She quickly swallowed the last of a hard-boiled egg and protested, "Yo're fergittin' 'bout Mrs. Farnham!"

"Oh!" Hildy exclaimed, jumping up so fast her lunch pail fell clattering to the ground. The round cover rolled away, reflecting the sun like a mirror. "You're right! Now what'll I do?"

"I dunno, less'n ye phone Mrs. Farnham."

"I couldn't do that!" Hildy said.

"Maybe ye could ask the principal to . . ."

"No!" Hildy shook her head hard, making her braids fly. "I'm already in enough trouble! Oh, I know! You could go to the Farnhams and tell them I'll be along as soon as possible."

"If'n Mizzus Farnham wanted me 'steada you, she'd a-said so."

"I'm sure she'll understand! Please do it for me!"

"Well, I reckon it won't do no harm."

"Oh, thank you!" Hildy reached over and gave her cousin a quick hug. "And while you're at the bus shed, make sure to tell Spud I'll get there soon as I can."

"Ye'll have to walk clean out to the Farnhams."

"We walked farther than that almost every day this summer. How about it? Will you do those things for me?"

Ruby reluctantly agreed, so Hildy continued through the afternoon with mixed feelings.

She was anxious to see Spud and try to talk him out of leaving Lone River, but there wouldn't be much time for that. However, it was very important.

After school, Hildy's mixed-up thoughts, loyalties and concerns helped her through the stern warning by Miss Krutz. "Hildy, you've exhibited very poor behavior so far today. It must stop at once! Do you understand that?"

"Yes, ma'm," Hildy replied, her mind focused more on Spud than her teacher.

"Very well! Here, take these erasers outside and smack them together to get the dust out of them. When you've finished, you may be excused."

When she had cleaned the erasers and was still sneezing from the eraser dust, Hildy grabbed her empty lunch pail and dashed across the dirt playground to the bus sheds. They were silent, their great open doors showing the vehicles were gone. There was only the smell of oil on dusty floors.

Hildy spun around, calling, "Spud?"

There was no answer. Hildy raced around the sheds, looking everywhere. She returned, breathless, to the open doors. Her head sagged in dismay.

Feeling miserable, Hildy started walking toward the city limits and the Farnham mansion in the country.

Hildy groaned within herself. *Spud's gone! And he didn't even say goodbye!*

CHAPTER
FIVE
—

A TERRIBLE DISCOVERY

Monday Afternoon

S ick at heart for having missed Spud, Hildy walked with head
down, deep in anguished thought. She reached the sidewalk
in front of the school. She heard a car pull to the curb beside
her.

Hildy glanced up and recognized the bright yellow 1929
Packard Victoria with black fenders, brown canvas top, and
whitewall balloon tires mounted on bright red spokes.

Looking at the driver, she exclaimed, "Brother Ben!"

Ben Strong sat straight and tall in the big car, just as he had
done on horseback many years ago as a Texas Ranger. Because
Hildy and he attended the same Lone River church, she knew
that he was a widower who had been ruined financially in Oklahoma's Dust Bowl before moving to California. Here he had
become fairly well-to-do by buying and selling range land.

His usually piercing blue eyes were now soft under the
shadow of his white cowboy hat, which hid a full head of totally
gray hair.

"Want a ride, Hildy?" he asked in his soft Texas drawl. He
gave his large white handlebar moustache a flip with the back
of his right forefinger.

"Oh, yes! Thank you!" Hildy exclaimed. She smiled her grat-itude while stepping onto the running board. She slid through the open right front passenger door onto the leather seat beside the six-foot, four-inch tall man.

He wore a clean blue work shirt buttoned at the sleeves. His jeans were faded blue above his highly polished brown cowboy boots.

Hildy said, "I'm late getting to Mrs. Farnham's! Could you drop me off there instead of at home?"

"Glad to oblige," Ben replied in his courtly manner.

As the car started to move, Hildy saw Ben glancing out of the corner of his eye at her disheveled clothes.

"Ruby got into a little scuffle at school, and I got involved," Hildy replied, gingerly touching the scratch on her cheek. She didn't feel like telling everything else that had gone on.

Ben seemed to sense that, and he was too much of a gentle-man to ask anything more. He changed the subject. "I came by earlier, hoping to catch you before the time for your bus. Ruby told me you were staying after school for something that wasn't your fault."

Hildy sighed. "It wasn't, but that didn't seem to make any difference to my teacher."

"Miss Krutz?"

Hildy asked in surprise, "You know her?"

"Everybody in Lone River knows everybody else. Poppy's really a nice woman, but her older brother keeps her under his thumb. Karl ran all her boyfriends off over the years. Now she's a rather bitter spinster."

Hildy found it hard to believe that the tall, stern woman had ever interested any man. But suddenly Hildy had a tiny new insight into her homeroom teacher.

Ben passed the city-limit sign, leaving the paved streets be-hind. The wheels crunched on the rural gravel road. He said, "Ruby told me Spud was back."

"You didn't see him?" Hildy asked, wondering if Ruby had delivered her message to Spud, asking him to wait.

"Nope. Just Ruby." Ben looked down at his passenger. "Were you surprised to see him?"

Hildy nodded and told about her brief conversation with Spud. She concluded, "I hoped that when Ruby explained why I was late, he'd still wait, but . . ." She didn't finish the sentence.

"If you're thinking he's already started for Chicago, I disagree with you, Hildy. He came three thousand miles to see you, but you two didn't finish your conversation. I suspect he's still around."

Hildy looked up eagerly at Ben's face, deeply lined by years of outdoor living. "You really think so?"

Ben smiled to encourage her. "Something must have come up so he couldn't wait, but I'm sure he'll be back."

"I sure hope you're right!"

They drove in silence for a mile or so before the old Ranger spoke again. "Some kids seem to get a raw deal out of life. Runaways—especially those who are abused or rejected at home—tend to end up in big trouble and have miserable lives."

"Spud's not like that!" Hildy said defensively, her voice rising.

"I didn't say he was, Hildy. But the fact remains that the odds are against any kid who doesn't get proper love and care at home. Rejection by those who should love you most seems to do something terrible to a kid. Why, some of the worst men I met in my days as a U.S. Marshal and Texas Ranger came from that kind of background."

"Spud's different!" Hildy insisted. "You once said he had the look of eagles in his eyes. Remember?"

"Yes, and I also said you had that same look. But you have a home where your family loves you, so you're going to draw on that as you get older. But Spud's never had any love and support in his home. I've lived long enough to see three and four generations of the same family. The sad truth is that most kids tend to be like their parents, because they're the models kids are around most. Unless something happens to break that cycle, it goes on for generations."

Ben paused, then added, "So I suspect the look in your eyes will always be there, always searching ahead and seeing things ordinary folks don't. But unless something happens to give

Spud love and hope, well, he could lose that look—and waste his whole life."

"Then we have to give him that love and hope!" Hildy said with feeling. "But how?"

"I've thought about that. Seems to me the best thing would be if somebody around here could apply to become his legal guardian. But it has to be fast, before he goes hoboing and we never see him again."

That terrible thought, and the hope that Brother Ben had offered, jerked Hildy up straight in the seat. "That makes sense!" she said with rising excitement. "People around here like Spud a lot! But everyone's so poor they couldn't raise another kid."

Suddenly, she had an idea. She exclaimed eagerly, "Brother Ben, you—"

He broke in quickly. "I'm nearly eighty-six, and might not always be here. Spud needs a younger guardian."

"But who?" Hildy asked, her mind racing. "Dad has all he can do to keep us kids fed. Ruby's father is not working regularly, and everybody's really poor."

"I'd say we ought to ask the Lord about that," Ben said as the Packard continued into the quiet countryside.

On the short drive to the mansion on the bluff overlooking the river, Hildy told Ben her feelings about the prejudice exhibited at school. It was something over which she had no control, yet she desperately needed that hundred-dollar scholarship. She concluded, "I'm off to such a bad start that it looks as if my chances of winning are pretty small, but I won't give up!"

"Atta girl!" Ben exclaimed. "There's an old saying that 'quitters never win, and winners never quit.' You've got to finish the race to win. Paul knew that."

"Paul?"

"The apostle. He was whipped, stoned, jailed, abandoned by friends, shipwrecked, and all sorts of other terrible things. Yet he could say: 'This one thing I do, forgetting those things which are behind, and reaching forth unto those things which are before . . .'"

"Oh, I remember! He said, 'I press toward the mark!' I guess that means the goal, huh?"

Ben nodded and slowed for the turn off the graveled county road onto the half mile of paved lane lined with palm trees. These led to a huge iron gate of black wrought iron set in the center of an eight-foot-high fence of smooth river stones. The fence stretched around the Farnham estate like a giant horse-shoe.

As the car stopped, Hildy slid out of the leather seat to open the gate. She was surprised to see that the padlock and heavy chain had been removed. It usually was looped around both right and left wings of the gate where they met in the center of the driveway.

"Guess Mr. Farnham's home from the bank," Hildy called to Ben as she pushed the right-hand section back on well-balanced hinges until it rested against a ten-foot-high wall of oleanders with pink blossoms.

The three-story frame home had been patterned after San Francisco's famous Victorians but modified since polio had con-fined Mrs. Farnham to a wheelchair and she could no longer climb stairs.

After Ben drove through, Hildy closed the gate and climbed back into the car. Ben pulled forward about a hundred yards past neat lawns, two persimmon trees, and rows of rosebushes. He stopped under a high porch that was open front and back. This had been the carriage entrance, where people used to stop out of the sun or rain when horses and buggies were common. To the left of this a few wooden steps led up to a large screened-in back porch that ran along the entire north side of the house.

Hildy saw Matthew Farnham through the screen as he opened the expensive mahogany door with its frosted-glass win-dow.

"Welcome!" he called, motioning for the new arrivals to come in. The banker was a small, natty man wearing a pale blue suit, white silk shirt, and dressy French tie.

Hildy had once told her father she thought it was strange that Mr. Farnham always wore both a belt and suspenders. Her father had said, "That's a banker for you. Always playing it safe!"

Matthew Farnham peered over the top of rectangular, silver-rimmed glasses and smiled in greeting as Hildy and Ben climbed out of the car. The men shook hands.

Hildy apologized for being late. She didn't mention her rumpled clothes or the scratch although she was aware that Mr. Farnham had noticed both. Hildy added quickly, "I hope nothing serious was wrong with Mrs. Farnham that she had to go to the doctor."

"Routine," the banker replied. "Having had polio means she has to see the doctor more than most folks, but she's already home, feeding some tramp at the back door."

That was a common thing for women to do in these hard times. Hildy's stepmother never turned away any hungry man from the barn-house, even though the Corrigans were as poor as anybody could be. Spud had told Hildy that while hoboing he often traded work for a meal.

Ben commented, "Matt, I'm surprised that anyone down on his luck would come into a grand place like this, even if the gate was unlocked."

The banker shrugged. "The country's full of men looking for work. They're called bums, tramps, bindlestiffs, and hobos. Sometimes they're accused of all kinds of terrible things—mostly theft. But I'm convinced most of those men are honest, just down on their luck.

"So, when the gate's open, once in awhile somebody does come to the back door. Beryl always feeds them, as most womenfolk do. She usually asks if they'll do a little work while she fixes a plate for them. The men are glad to cut wood, clean out the barn, or do something in exchange for a bite. Helps them keep their dignity."

Hildy asked, "Where's Ruby? I'll go relieve her and take care of Dickie and Connie."

"She's playing with them out by the barn."

As Hildy started alongside the house, Ben called, "If Ruby wants a ride to her house, tell her I'll wait."

Hildy nodded. As she approached the open kitchen window,

she saw Mrs. Farnham in her wheelchair taking a pot of stew off the range. Hildy's employer never let her handicap keep her from cooking and other household chores she'd handled before the crippling polio struck. Beryl Farnham didn't have a full-time hired girl, but relied on Hildy and Ruby for help.

Mrs. Farnham looked up and smiled. "Oh, there you are!" she said through the screen. She wheeled the chair toward the window. Her left leg was thin as a broom handle under her print dress. She glanced at Hildy's clothes and cheek. "Ruby told me about your delay. Is everything all right now?"

"Yes, ma'm."

Mrs. Farnham was a small-framed woman, fragile as a china doll, with blonde hair. Tiny blue veins showed under the surface of her almost transparent white skin. Her face was lined, and she had dark circles under her eyes.

Hildy said, "I'll go take care of the children as soon as I change."

Hildy hurried to the large hall closet and changed into old shoes and a dress she kept there. Ruby also kept boys' clothing there, including a hat and old shoes. Then Hildy ran across the well-tended lawn toward the barn. She heard the ring of an ax behind the woodshed and guessed that was the tramp earning a meal. Hildy glanced at him as she passed. His back was turned, yet he seemed vaguely familiar. Hildy shrugged and hurried on. She called, "Ruby, Dickie, Connie! I'm here."

Two children dashed out of the barn, happily yelling greetings to Hildy. Ruby followed at a walk.

Dickie was fair with large blue eyes and masses of yellow curls. His sister's hair was straight and so blonde it was almost white. Her eyes were not as large as her brother's, but they were every bit as blue.

Hildy knelt and swept the children into her arms. "Sorry I'm late," she said. "But I'll make it up to you. Want me to swing you?"

"Me first!" the boy cried.

Connie's face puckered in disappointment. "I wanted to be first!"

"You let your brother do it this time, and I'll give you a special treat later," Hildy said. "Okay?"

When Connie agreed, Hildy relayed Ben's message to Ruby. She ran toward the house for a ride home.

Connie sought the shade of a gnarled old fig tree while Hildy approached Dickie. He was already seated on the swing under the deep shade of a silver maple.

After a dozen pushes of the swing, Hildy announced it was Connie's turn. She helped the boy down and turned toward the fig tree, but Connie wasn't there.

"Connie?" Hildy called, looking around. "Where are you? Time for your ride."

When there was no answer, Dickie suggested, "Maybe she went back to the barn."

"Let's go see," Hildy replied, taking the boy's hand. She hurried across the lawn, surprised at how quickly a little girl could disappear. She thought of the bluff above the river, but knew there hadn't been time for Connie to get that far.

Hildy became aware that she was no longer hearing the ring of ax on wood. She turned with Dickie toward the woodshed. "I hear her!" Hildy exclaimed.

Hildy and the boy rounded the woodshed. Connie was sitting on an old stump used as a chopping block. She was talking to the woodcutter, whose back was toward Hildy.

"Connie!" Hildy called. "It's your turn to . . ."

She stopped as the little girl and the man turned to look at her. Hildy's heart did a flip-flop.

It's him! she told herself, memory flooding her body with fear. *He's the man who chased Ruby and me in the river bottom!*

CHAPTER Six

BAD NEWS KEEPS COMING

Monday Afternoon

For a moment, Hildy stared at the stoutly built, unwashed and unshaven tramp. Goosebumps rippled up and down Hildy's arms as she remembered how he and his dog had chased her and Ruby at the river yesterday.

The tramp's brown eyes seemed to regard Hildy thoughtfully, as if he were trying to place her.

"Whatcha staring at?" he demanded in a raspy voice.

"Uh—nothing! I just came to bring her in." Hildy reached out suddenly and grabbed Connie's arm. "Come on!"

Connie let out a childish wail of protest. "Not now! He's going to make me a whistle out of an old stick."

Hildy didn't reply, but reached down, scooped the four-year-old into her arms, and hurried away.

When the woodshed was between her and the man, Hildy set Connie down, then knelt to peer into her face. "Didn't your mother teach you not to talk to strangers?"

"Yes, but Mommy talked to him, so why can't I?"

"Maybe you'd better let your mother explain."

Hildy hurried toward the house, calling for Dickie to join them. Hildy had a strong desire to look back and see if the tramp was watching, but she didn't turn around. *Maybe he didn't recognize me*, she told herself.

As Hildy and the Farnham children approached the mansion's back door, Hildy wished Ruby were here to share the discovery. But a glance at the side of the house showed that Ben's car was gone. Ruby must have gone with him. Hildy hurried the children onto the screened-in back porch and into the kitchen.

From her wheelchair, Mrs. Farnham reached over the table to place a tin cup of hot black coffee onto a large plate. It already held two biscuits and a bowl of stew.

"Oh, Hildy, I'm glad you came in. Would you mind calling that poor man out there? His food's ready."

Hildy hesitated. "Mrs. Farnham, could I talk to you alone for a minute first, please?"

"Something wrong?" she asked, glancing anxiously at Hildy, then at the children.

Hildy turned to the them and asked, "Would you two go in the parlor and find some books? I'll read to you in just a moment."

When Dickie and Connie had gone, Hildy closed the door behind them and turned to face her employer.

"Hildy, what on earth's the matter?" Mrs. Farnham exclaimed.

"Have you ever seen that tramp before?" Hildy asked.

"Well, I'm not sure, but he looks like a man who asked for food a couple of weeks ago. Why do you ask?"

"Maybe I shouldn't say anything, Mrs. Farnham, but I *know* I've seen him before." Hildy quickly related the incident at the river bottom.

When Hildy had finished, Mrs. Farnham propelled her wheelchair away from the table. "You girls probably just startled him, and he naturally reacted by yelling. When he came to our door, he seemed like a nice man. I'm sure he's harmless."

"He did more than yell at us!" Hildy reminded her employer.

"He chased us and set his big dog on us!"

Mrs. Farnham removed old flatware from a top drawer and placed knife, fork, and spoon on the plate. "You're sure it was the same man?" When Hildy nodded, the woman added, "That does make me a little nervous, of course. But we'll feed him, and he'll be on his way. I don't expect we'll ever see him again. Now, would you mind taking this plate out to him?"

Hildy didn't want to see the man up close again, but she had no choice. She said, "Yes, ma'm," and carried the food and coffee across the back porch. The stranger stood on the top step, trying to peer through the rusted screen door. Hildy opened it just enough to reach the plate out to him.

He took it but looked at her through the screen. "You live here?" he asked in a gravelly voice.

Hildy shook her head and closed the screen door, returning to the kitchen without saying anything more. But when she sat down to read with Dickie on one side and Connie on the other, gooseflesh still rippled up and down her arms. That sensation passed only when she saw the tramp walking past the rose-bushes toward the gate, wiping his mouth with the back of a dirty hand.

It was nearing dusk when Hildy's work was done for the day. She started walking home, stopping to loop the chain around both ends of the iron gate and snap the padlock behind her. She hurried down the lane and onto the country road. She had done that many times before, but this time she glanced nervously at every tree, every bush. Everything made a shadow where the stranger could be waiting for her.

She wondered, *Did Ruby see him while she was here? No, she must not have, or she'd have mentioned it.*

Just before full darkness, Hildy reached the Lombardy poplars and turned onto the dusty lane leading up to the barn-house. She let out a big sigh of relief both for safely reaching home and seeing Uncle Nate's borrowed, topless Model T parked there. That meant Ruby was there too.

Hildy thought, *I wonder if that means Uncle Nate's made a decision about moving to the Ozarks. Anyway, I'll get to tell Ruby about seeing that man again.*

Hildy quickly opened the door and stepped inside. Ruby, Uncle Nate, and Molly were seated on the homemade wooden benches around the kitchen table with its cracked oilcloth cover.

"Hildy!" Ruby exclaimed, "Yo're jist in time to try talkin' muh daddy into stayin' here, 'steada takin' that old church job in the Ozarks!"

Nate Konning was a tall, slender man with blond hair and a glistening of day-old beard the same color. He wore a pair of scuffed cowboy boots and a brown suit Hildy knew had once belonged to a man who had died. The family had given Nate the suit. Her uncle was so broke he wore it whenever he went to church or had an opportunity to preach. He did that part time when he wasn't doing manual labor at a nearby ranch.

He said softly, "Now Ruby honey, I done tol' ye I'm a-gonna do what I feel led to do, an' they ain't nothin' you, Hildy ner nobody . . ." He paused, frowning. Then he managed a wan grin at Hildy. "Reckon when I git—get worked up some, I plumb—I mean, I forget what you tol' me about speaking good English."

Hildy smiled encouragement. "You're doing fine, Uncle Nate. Remember, the first thing in changing something is to be aware you're doing it, and then really want to change how you talk."

"Much obliged," Nate replied. "I shore—sure wouldn't want to dishonor our Lord by not speakin' proper English, seein' as how I'm His representative an' all."

Hildy was bursting to tell Ruby the news about the stranger, but she didn't want to alarm the rest of her family. So she forced herself to sit down beside her cousin and look across at her uncle. "Does that mean you've made up your mind to accept the call to the Ozark church?" she asked.

"No, I'm thinkin' a powerful lot about it, but until I'm sure, I'm not a-gonna—not going to do anything."

Hildy exchanged relieved glances with her cousin. She didn't want Ruby to move away, either. Hildy could now focus on the other thing on her mind. She said, "Ruby, could you come with me?"

The girls walked outside. Full darkness had fallen. Invisible crickets were starting their nightly orchestrations. In the distance, a bullfrog gave his deep-throated call from an irrigation ditch.

"Ruby!" Hildy exclaimed when they were away from the barn-house far enough that nobody could see them. "Did you get a good look at the man chopping wood at the Farnham's?"

"The tramp? Not really. Why?"

"Well, I saw him, and he's the same one who chased us with his dog at the river!"

"Ye shore?"

Hildy nodded emphatically and recounted what had happened at the mansion after Ruby left with Brother Ben. She concluded, "I don't think he recognized me."

"Even if he did," Ruby replied, "he won't bother ye none whilst yo're a-workin' there. Nor them little kids. 'Sides, mosta the time the gate's locked so's he couldn't git in. An ye don't work thar at night now that school's started."

Hildy tried to be reassured by those words, but there was a little nagging fear at the back of her mind. It wouldn't go away, not even after the conversation shifted to Spud.

Why hadn't he waited for her after school? Hildy wondered. She hoped he hadn't started for Chicago. Could somebody around Lone River be found who'd care enough about Spud to become his guardian?

Ruby and her father had been gone only a few minutes when Joe Corrigan arrived home. His family met him with the question uppermost in their minds. Elizabeth asked it as he came through the door. "Did you get laid off, Daddy?"

Her father looked very tired, Hildy thought, as he reached down and hugged Elizabeth and her younger sisters to his huge chest. "No, not yet anyway."

Hildy took his cowboy hat and hung it on a spike driven into a two-by-four by the door. "Any idea when you'll know for sure?"

Joe shook his head, but Hildy caught a kind of knowing look pass between her father and stepmother. It gave Hildy an uneasy feeling, but she knew better than to say anything more.

After a supper of boiled beans, biscuits, and gravy, when all the other kids had gone to sleep, Hildy sat at the kitchen table with her father and stepmother.

Joe stared silently into the lamp for a long time. That raised Hildy's anxiety because her mind was already filling with old memories. She couldn't remember how often she'd heard her father say he'd lost his job and he'd have to go looking for another. In these hard times of Depression, some men were always out of a job, even good men. Yet Joe Corrigan always managed to find something. To do that, he frequently left his family behind and went job hunting alone, because it was cheaper. When he found work—often in another state—his family rejoined him. They lived in whatever housing they could get, usually shacks.

But Hildy had a dream to change all that. Shortly after her mother died and her father was off someplace looking for work, Hildy's little sisters were crying. They were scared, alone, and unable to understand all that had happened to make their young lives so miserable.

In that dark hour, with Ruby listening, Hildy had made a promise to her four little sisters and baby brother. "Someday we'll have a 'forever' home, one where we never, ever have to move again."

That vision had kept the children going, especially since arriving in Lone River this summer. Hildy felt that someday around Lone River they'd find that 'forever' home. But now the dream was threatened again.

So she sat, hurting inside with the uncertainty, absently petting the raccoon curled up in her lap.

Finally, her father spoke in a subdued tone. "If I'm laid off, we'll move to Grass Valley."

Hildy stopped petting Mischief. "Grass Valley?" she repeated. "Where's that?"

" 'Bout a hundred and fifty miles from here, up in the Mother Lode Country. The gold mines are in full operation. Fact is, I hear tell they don't even know there's a Depression on. Why, I heard that hardrock miners make $3.50 to $4.00 a day. That's more'n $90.00 a month for a six-day week, while I just make $60.00."

"Oh, Daddy!" Hildy cried in dismay. "I don't want to move away from Lone River! I don't even want to change schools, because then I couldn't win that hundred dollars!"

Joe Corrigan's jaw muscles twitched before he reached over and gently laid a rough hand on his daughter's. "I know, Hildy," he replied in a soft tone, "but there are no other jobs around here. So if I'm laid off, I have to find work wherever I can— maybe Grass Valley." He sighed and added, "I'm sorry about the scholarship."

Hildy wanted to yell, "Being sorry won't help!" but she kept quiet, knowing her father was right. Instead, she got up and lightly lifted his hand to her cheek. "I know, Daddy," she said. "I know."

Saddened and discouraged, Hildy fought back tears as she hurried across the barn-house. A screen had been stretched there for privacy, because the barn-house was one large room. The screen was made of an old quilt hung over a clothesline and held in place by clothespins. Hildy ducked behind it to change into her nightgown. Mischief waddled after her, complaining at being left behind.

Hildy reached down and scooped up her pet, cuddling her close. "Mischief," Hildy whispered, "if we move away, maybe they won't allow raccoons! I couldn't stand that, Mischief! I couldn't!"

Hildy made her way to the pallet where she slept. She lay down with Mischief beside her. Hildy closed her eyes to pray, but instead, all her difficulties raced through her mind, each adding weight to her already heavy heart.

There're the scholarship problems with Miss Krutz, Zelpha, and her friends. Has Spud gone away without saying goodbye? I don't want Ruby and Uncle Nate to move to the Ozarks. I don't want to move away from Lone River. I've got to win that scholarship. That tramp makes me uneasy. Ruby's right—This is going to be a terrible year!

Then Hildy checked herself. *That's no way for a Christian to think!* she scolded herself. She tried to think of a helpful verse memorized in Sunday school. One seemed appropriate: "What things soever ye desire, when ye pray, believe that ye receive them, and ye shall have them."

Hildy took a slow, deep breath, let it out, and began her silent prayers. Then, feeling better in spite of knowing her problems weren't over, she slept.

Chapter Seven

DANGER AT DUSK

Tuesday

As Hildy had so often found, her faith was promptly tested. She awoke with a sense of doubt. *Maybe things won't work out! I'll lose the scholarship and . . . Stop that!* She turned back the demons of doubt by reading her Bible, praying, and remembering something she'd read: *How do you strengthen your faith? By exercise, the same as muscles are developed, through resistance. Faith grows by testing.*

Feeling better, Hildy was promptly rewarded on the bus when Zelpha ignored her and Ruby and didn't pick on them. At school the cousins let Zelpha off first. She was met by Edna and Tessie. All three girls hurried away without any snide remarks directed at Hildy or Ruby.

The cousins started across the school grounds when someone called Hildy's name. She turned to where a boy in an aviator cap was leaving the shade of a sycamore tree growing at the curb.

"Spud!" Hildy exclaimed.

Ruby made a snorting noise of disapproval. She walked on, saying, "See ye in homeroom, Hildy."

Spud hurried up, grinning at Hildy. "Hi," he said.

"What happened to you yesterday?" Hildy asked.

"I came here a little before lunch to wait for you, but the truant officer saw me. He chased me, but I ran away. Then he hung around the school all afternoon, so I didn't dare risk trying to meet you again."

"Aren't you afraid he'll catch you this morning? I mean, being so close to school?"

"No, I saw him across town near the Southside School awhile ago. I'm safe here."

"Don't you get tired of having to run all the time?"

"Keeps me in good shape," Spud replied with a grin.

One great question nagged at Hildy's mind, but she didn't want to ask it for fear it would bring a reply she didn't want. Instead of asking if he was leaving for Chicago, she asked, "Where'd you stay last night?"

"Ben Strong saw me as he was driving back from dropping you off at the Farnhams' and taking Ruby home. I accepted his hospitality for the night."

"Did—did he say anything about what he and I talked about?"

"Like what?"

"Well, if you'll stay here for a while, maybe we can find someone who might become your legal guardian. Then you wouldn't have to go hoboing and waste your life."

Hildy saw at once that it was the wrong thing to say. Spud's face clouded. "I don't need a guardian! I'm not wasting my life, and I can take care of myself. Besides, I like hoboing."

"Please don't be angry! It's just that I—so many of us care what happens to you. We want to help."

"I don't need anybody's help!" Spud said, pulling himself upright and puffing out his chest a little. "I've already been a bindlestiff for a couple years and . . ."

An outside bell rang loudly from the school building. Hildy exclaimed, "There's the first bell! I don't dare be late again! But I can't let you go off angry. Come back at lunch."

"I was going to start for Chicago this . . ." he began.

"Oh, please don't do that!" Hildy stopped, flustered and

embarrassed. "I mean, not until we've had a chance to talk some more. See you at lunch?"

Spud hesitated, frowning in thought. Then he nodded, "If the truant officer isn't around, I'll be there."

"And if he is, how about after school? By the bus sheds before I leave for the Farnhams'?"

"It'll make me late starting east, but I guess so."

Hildy smiled, waved goodbye, and dashed across the dusty school grounds, up the steep stairs, and down the nearly empty halls of the old red-brick building. She slid into her seat just as the final bell clanged.

Miss Krutz managed a frosty smile. "For a moment there, I thought you weren't going to make it, Hildy."

The class tittered, but the teacher rapped for attention with her ruler and called the roll. When she had finished, she asked, "How many of you saw the Navy's dirigible when it flew over Lone River yesterday?"

Almost every hand went up, including Hildy's.

Miss Krutz nodded approvingly. "How many of you would like to see one of them up close?"

Again, there was an instant forest of upraised hands and some excited exclamations of agreement.

"Very well," the teacher continued. "Through the generosity of Mr. Emery Stanway, a field trip has been arranged for this class to visit the dirigible base at Sunnyvale a week from this coming Saturday."

A chorus of surprised and delighted exclamations erupted from the class. Hildy was suddenly excited too, in spite of her other concerns.

Miss Krutz added, "Naturally, we shall have to prepare for that trip in order to have some special knowledge about dirigibles before we see one up close. You can utilize that information in your essays."

Hildy liked writing essays and compositions, but she knew she'd have to write a very good one because of Zelpha's obvious advantage with the scholarship judges.

Miss Krutz held up a stack of magazine and newspaper clippings about dirigibles. She said students could consult her materials, as well as those in the class library, the town's small public library, or any other resources they could find.

"There's one thing more," the teacher concluded, her eyes sweeping the room. "Anyone whose deportment is less than exemplary will not be allowed to go on the field trip. Unacceptable behavior will also adversely affect a student in the essay competition. Is that clear?"

Miss Krutz's eyes seemed to linger longer on Hildy and Ruby, but Hildy didn't care. She had made up her mind to win that scholarship. Now she had the increased excitement of being able to see a dirigible up close after researching something about them.

Hildy was anxious to talk with Spud, so when lunchtime came, she grabbed her lunch pail and ran outside. Ruby followed at a leisurely pace. But Spud wasn't anywhere around.

Not again! Hildy groaned inwardly. Then she swallowed her disappointment and turned back to meet Ruby. Hildy said, "He'll be here after school."

"Maybe," Ruby replied. "Or maybe he done took off fer Chicago, and ye won't never see him ag'in!"

"Don't say that!" Hildy replied sharply.

Still, that fear haunted her as she led the way to an unoccupied bench. The cousins pried the shiny lids off their pails just as Hildy heard a familiar sound.

Ruby also heard it. "That's muh daddy's ol' car a-comin'!" She jumped up and headed for the curb.

Hildy followed, knowing it was unusual for any parent to come to the school during the day.

The old topless Model T wheezed into silence. Both girls anxiously leaned over the driver's side door.

Nate Konning explained the reason for his visit. "How would you two gals like to take a ride up to Thunder Mountain this Saturday?"

Ruby exclaimed, "Kin we see Mizzus Benton and all her kids?"

Hildy noticed a teasing little smile tugging at the corners of his mouth as he answered, "Well, maybe."

Hildy asked, "Why're you going there, Uncle Nate?"

"While I was wrestling with a decision about accepting that call to the Ozark church or staying here, I felt led to go visit Thunder Mountain."

The girls exchanged knowing looks. Both Hildy and Ruby suspected Nate was more than casually interested in a widow named Lotta Benton, who lived at Thunder Mountain.

Ruby sometimes did light housework for the Farnhams on Saturday, but eagerly agreed to go with her father instead. Hildy explained that she'd be working at the Farnhams' and couldn't ride along into the Mother Lode.

Her uncle said he was sorry to hear that, and he'd pick Ruby up at the Corrigans' after work. He drove off.

Ruby turned to Hildy and grabbed both her forearms. "Ye know whut that means, huh? He's a-gittin' kinda sweet on Mizzus Benton! Maybe he'll up an' marry her, and then I'll have me a whole passel of ready-made brothers and sisters! Best of all, I reckon he'd have to stay here, 'steada goin' back to them Ozarks!"

Hildy returned to her lunch pail. "I want you to be happy, but even if he does marry her, there's not enough money for a full-time pastor at that little Thunder Mountain church."

"Then he kin work part time aroun' Lone River, like some other preacher men do! Hildy, I tell ye, I think that Ozark job's good as fergotten!"

Hildy started to caution Ruby, but looked up and lowered her voice. "Here comes Zelpha and her friends. Don't do or say anything to cause trouble!"

Ruby bristled. "I ain't skeered o' them! I kin whup them all at once with one hand tied behind my back!"

"If you don't care about yourself, think about me! I have to win that scholarship, and I won't if I get into any more trouble."

Ruby seemed to consider that. She relaxed. "Yeah, reckon so. 'Sides, I'd like to go see them thar dur-juh-bulls Miss Krutz tol' us about."

The cousins avoided making eye contact with the three other

girls. They walked by, giggling, but didn't say anything or even look directly at Hildy and Ruby.

Hildy said, "Maybe they're losing interest in picking on us."

"More'n likely they're jist a-bidin' their time. It ain't over yet."

Hildy thought that was probably right, but she breathed a sigh of relief that at least things were quiet for now.

All during the afternoon, as Hildy changed classes and teachers, she worried that Spud wouldn't be waiting after school. When the final dismissal bell rang, Hildy tried not to run toward the bus sheds, but she was so eager that only Ruby's teasing remarks made Hildy walk slowly enough so the two girls arrived together.

Their old, high-topped red bus was lined up with some of the newer, lower yellow ones. Students drifted toward their buses.

Ruby glanced around and said, "Spud ain't here."

Hildy's eager search had already confirmed that. "Maybe he's with Brother Ben," she said, looking hopefully in all directions.

"Or maybe he lit out fer Chicago." Ruby's voice plainly indicated that was fine with her.

"He might show up before our bus leaves," Hildy said hopefully. "We'll wait and get on last."

Spud didn't appear, so finally the cousins boarded the bus. They sat well away from Zelpha, who again ignored them.

Ruby whispered, "I bet she's a-dreamin' up some devilment, makin' us think she's lost interest. Jist when we relax, she'll whang us with somethin' turr'ble."

Hildy tried to put that thought out of her mind, but it was still there, a nagging concern, when the bus stopped at the end of the Farnhams' long driveway. Hildy said she'd see Ruby at the barn-house, and left the bus. She hurried to the gate. It was unlocked. As she let herself in, she heard both Dickie and Connie crying hard.

Wonder what's the matter with them" she asked herself, breaking into a run.

Near the carriage entrance, Hildy saw through the screened-in porch that her employer was sitting in her wheelchair just inside the frontroom door.

Mrs. Farnham called, "Oh, Hildy! I'm glad you're here. Come in, come in!"

There was an urgent tone in the woman's voice. Hildy hurried up the few steps and through the screen door. "What's wrong?"

Mrs. Farnham swung her wheelchair around. "That man, the tramp you saw here yesterday, came back today, looking for another handout and . . ."

"He didn't hurt Connie or Dickie?" Hildy interrupted anxiously.

"Oh, no!" Mrs. Farnham wheeled her chair into the house and across a rich Persian rug in the entryway. She stopped at the bottom of the stairs. "I asked him to sweep out the barn while I fixed him some food. A little later, I heard our old horse neighing and kicking the barn walls."

Hildy glanced through the open kitchen door toward the barn, where Robin was stabled. Robin was a gentle gray mare that was at least twenty years old. Mr. Farnham kept her because she was the only thing he owned back when he was dirt poor and just starting to build his career.

Mrs. Farnham continued. "Matt wasn't home, so I sent Dickie to see if the man was all right. Dickie came running back, terrified. He said the tramp was poking a pitchfork at Robin!"

Hildy's mouth dropped open. "Why?"

"I wondered that myself, but I couldn't roll the chair out there, and Dickie was too upset to send him out again. So I called from the back door until the man heard me. When he came out of the barn, I asked why he was using the pitchfork on the horse. He said Robin kicked at him, so he was teaching her a lesson."

"Oh, Mrs. Farnham, I can't believe it!"

"I know Robin didn't kick at him, so I told him to get off our property and never come back!"

Hildy knelt to put her arms around the woman. "He—he didn't hurt you, did he?"

Mrs. Farnham shook her head, her eyes misty. "No, but when he was going down the lane, he turned around and yelled back, saying we'd all be sorry, *real* sorry!"

Hildy tried to comfort Mrs. Farnham by saying the tramp didn't really mean that. However, as Hildy went upstairs to comfort the children, she felt uneasy.

If he meant it, she asked herself, *what would he do? And would he also do something to Ruby—or me?*

Remembering the way the tramp had looked at her when she handed him his food, Hildy shivered.

CHAPTER EIGHT

TENSION ON EVERY SIDE

Tuesday Afternoon

The children had stopped crying as Hildy reached the second floor and looked down the long carpeted hallway. It was dimly lit, even in daylight, because it was an inside hall with three closed bedroom doors on each side. A tall, narrow window at the far end gave the only light.

Hildy called, "Dickie! Connie! It's Hildy! Where are you?"

For a moment, there was no answer. Hildy's eyes swept the six bedroom doors of dark wood. She knew that each room was fully furnished. Each had outside windows for light and ventilation. None was used since Mrs. Farnham's polio prevented her from climbing stairs.

She and her husband had remodeled the house and now used what had originally been a maid's downstairs bedroom. It was off the parlor and near the carriage entrance. A spacious screened-in porch on the south side of the house, opposite the carriage entrance, had been remodeled to make separate rooms for Dickie and Connie. But when they were upset, Hildy knew the children preferred their old bedrooms upstairs.

She opened the door to the boy's former room. He was sprawled face down on the high bed. It had ornate metal head and footboards. His sister glumly sat in an old rocking chair with an upholstered red and gold padded velour seat and mahogany back with gold oriental decorations. Hildy had often rocked the children in this chair.

"Your mother told me what happened," Hildy began, sitting down on the edge of the bed. "It's all right," she added, reaching out to touch each child.

The boy raised his head and looked out of eyes red from crying. "That ol' tramp hurt Robin!" Dickie exclaimed with a sob. "He was mean! And he yelled at Mommy and us!"

Connie slid out of the chair and into the circle of Hildy's arms. "He said he'd do bad things to us too!"

"It'll be all right," Hildy repeated. "Here, let me sit in the rocker and hold you both for a while. Sometimes holding's the nicest feeling in the whole world."

The six-year-old boy was quite a lapful by himself, but the chair was large, and Hildy managed to squeeze both children into the rocker. She rocked gently, urging brother and sister to talk about their pain and fear. Then Hildy reassured them with soothing words. Finally, she began singing softly.

When the children had been silent for some time, Hildy slowly stopped rocking. She bent her head to see if they were asleep. The boy's eyes were closed, but Connie looked up at Hildy.

"You sure that man won't hurt us?"

"Of course he won't!" Hildy hugged Connie tightly and laid her cheek alongside the child's. "Forget him!"

Connie said wistfully, "I wish you lived here with us. Mommy can't go fast in her chair, and she can't go up or down stairs or out in the yard much. And Daddy has to go to work."

"I wish I could stay too, but I can't."

Connie sat up suddenly. "I hear my daddy's car coming! Mommy phoned him after that man yelled at us." The little girl slid off of Hildy's lap. "I love you," she said, giving Hildy a quick kiss on the cheek.

Hildy was moved, but before she could say anything, Connie darted out of the room, down the hallway toward the stairs. Hildy managed to stand up on cramped legs. She tried to ease the boy onto the bed without waking him, but he opened his eyes and heard Connie yelling "Daddy!" Hildy took the boy's hand and led him downstairs.

A few minutes later, while Hildy stood quietly in the background, the banker sat in an overstuffed sofa. He held a child on each knee and listened in silence to his wife's account of what the tramp had done and said.

Finally Mr. Farnham said, "It probably was just an idle threat. But just in case it wasn't, I'll keep the gate locked. I'll also ask the sheriff to have a patrol car keep an eye on the place."

He looked at Hildy where she stood leaning against the side of a fine, old china hutch. "I think my wife and children need to get out of the house for a while. So if you'll help me get them into the car, I'll drop you off at your home and take my family for a little outing."

It was late afternoon when the Farnhams' Pierce Arrow stopped in front of the barn-house. Hildy was a little surprised that her younger sisters didn't come rushing out. The Corrigans didn't have much company, so when the little girls heard a car coming, they always hurried outside to see who it was.

Hildy waved goodbye to the Farnhams and hurried to the barn door. Inside, she heard her baby brother crying.

Hildy opened the door. "I'm home."

Her stepmother looked up from where she was sending a wooden rolling pin back and forth across a mass of biscuit dough on the kitchen table. Flour covered her arms to the elbow, and she had smudges on her cheeks.

"You're home early!" Molly commented, using the back of her left hand to brush a lock of hair out of her eyes.

Hildy started to explain what had happened at the Farnhams', but Molly spoke again. "Would you check Joey? I think he wants his diedy changed, and I can't stop until I finish this, or the dough will be ruined."

"Sure," Hildy said, stooping down to pet her raccoon as it

waddled from the lug box den to greet her. She asked, "Where are the kids?"

"They're all over at the neighbors' across the pasture. When Elizabeth and Martha came home from school, they wanted to go play with them, so I said okay. Then Sarah and Iola set up such a fuss I let them go along. Joey was asleep, and I thought I could manage, but now he's awake and letting us know he's not happy."

Hildy put the coon down and bent over her sixteen-month-old brother. "What's the matter, Joey?" she asked in a soothing tone. "You got a wet diaper?"

Hildy picked up some old rags that had been washed and cut to be used as diapers. She started changing Joey, smiling at him. He stopped crying and smiled back.

Molly asked, "You see Spud today?"

"No," Hildy said around the closed safety pins she held loosely in her lips.

"He's a strange boy," Molly said.

"How do you mean?" Hildy asked a little more sharply than she had intended.

"Don't get upset, Hildy! I just mean he's so smart, yet his life's a mess." Molly returned to rolling out the dough. "Do you realize how special a friend you are to him? He came all the way from Brooklyn to tell you goodbye."

Hildy considered that in silence, pinning the diaper.

Molly added, "Good friendships are rare—ones that last, I mean. In fact, I suspect most people are lucky to have one good friend. You've got two—Ruby and Spud."

"Ruby and I've been friends for years, but maybe now she's going to move away. Spud's already gone, I guess."

"Friends stay friends, even if they're far apart."

"Maybe so," Hildy said, picking up Joey, "but it sure hurts more when they're far away."

Hildy didn't want to talk about that anymore, so she placed her brother on his pallet and told Molly about the tramp's threat to the Farnhams. Hildy thought about telling Molly that the same man had chased Ruby and her at the river, but she heard

Elizabeth and her other sisters coming home across the pasture. At the same time, Hildy heard Uncle Nate's Model T stop outside.

Ruby ran in. "Hildy, we'uns got to talk private!"

Molly said she could spare Hildy for a while now that the other girls were home to help with Joey and with supper. Ruby's father said he'd help too, so Hildy and Ruby hurried outside.

When they were just out of earshot of the barn-house, Ruby turned to Hildy, her eyes glowing. "Ye know what muh daddy asked me when I got home from school?"

Before Hildy could reply, Ruby rushed on. "He asked me if'n I ever wanted a brother or sister! Naturally, I tol' him I'd admire having a whole passel of 'em! Ye know what that means, Hildy? Do ye?"

"You think he's seriously thinking about marrying Mrs. Benton, right?"

"Right! She's done got four kids younger'n me!"

"That would be wonderful, but it might not work out. I mean, I hope it does. But don't get your hopes up."

"There ye go ag'in!" Ruby flared, stopping in the middle of the lane by the poplars. "Throwin' cold water!"

"No, I'm not! I said it would be wonderful. Sure, I admit I wouldn't want you to move away, but I'd rather have you happy by getting the family you've always wanted. I just don't want you to get hurt if it doesn't work out."

Ruby's little flare-up eased. "Jist the same," she said in a softer tone, "when me'n muh daddy git back from Thunder Mountain, ye might need to start gittin' ready fer a weddin'!"

The cousins walked out onto the graveled county road. Hildy told what Mrs. Farnham had said about the tramp.

When she finished, Ruby said, "I don't like the sounds of it—nary a bit! I didn't like it none when he sicced his dawg on us and chased us! Now he's a-pokin' an ol' hoss with a pitchfork and yellin' at a crippled lady in a wheelchair—not to mention little kids!"

The cousins discussed the situation at some length until they came to the iron-girder bridge across the river.

Hildy stopped and inhaled deeply. "Umm! Smell the cotton-woods? And the willows? Look how pretty the trees are with the sun hitting them! I love to see the leaves change color."

"Shore is a purdy sight," Ruby agreed.

"Peaceful too," Hildy replied. She looked over the acres of valley oaks that spread across the bottom land before they gave way to the cottonwoods and willows that grew nearer the water. "I guess there's not much else in the world more peaceful than a river in the country this time of year."

"This one could be dangerous," Ruby replied. "That tramp might be down here, a-watchin' us."

Hildy waved her hand toward the distant bend in the river where brown cornstalks stood tall and dry on the level acreage above it. "He was away down there. Let's just walk along this end, near the road."

Ruby shook her head. "Nuh-uh! Maybe his old striped dawg is a-runnin' loose somewheres down thar! 'Sides, it's soon gonna be dark!"

For a moment Hildy hesitated. Then she sighed heavily. "Well, you can stay up here, but I'm going to enjoy some of that peace and quiet for a few minutes."

"Ye mean yo're a-gonna git off alone somewheres so's ye kin think about Spud!"

Hildy had pushed thoughts of the boy into the back of her mind, but the mention of him caused a sudden sad and lonely feeling. *Why didn't he show up today as he promised? Has he really left for Chicago?*

Hildy started easing down the steep narrow path at the edge of the rusted iron bridge. "I won't be long," she called over her shoulder.

Ruby muttered, "In that case, reckon I may's well go along." She followed Hildy down to the river bottom.

The cousins walked under the great valley oaks that grew inland from the river. Ruby asked, "Ye want to talk about him? Jist 'cause him 'n' me don't always git along don't mean I don't unnerstand that he means a lot to ye."

"He's a good friend," Hildy replied, thinking of what Molly

had said. "I didn't want him to leave any more than I'd want you and Uncle Nate to move away. I just don't know why Spud didn't show up today."

Ruby suddenly tensed. "Shh!" She reached out to clutch Hildy's arm. "I heerd somethin'!"

Hildy stiffened and listened, aware of how fast darkness was falling and how far they were from the road. She caught a low "whoof!" from willows growing by the river.

Ruby whispered, "That's his dawg! Let's git outta here!" She turned toward the road.

A male voice called out of the dusk. "Hey!"

"It's him!" Ruby cried. "He's a-comin'!" She started running.

The voice came again from deep shadows behind some willows by the river. "Hey!"

Memories flashed through Hildy's mind. The stranger and his dog chasing them. Threats made to a defenseless, handicapped mother and her little children. The stern warning the stranger had given Hildy and Ruby if he ever saw them down here again.

Hildy whirled away from the willows. She called, "I'm right behind you!" and raced after Ruby.

Chapter Nine

A STORY AND A CHALLENGE

Tuesday and Wednesday

Hildy ran hard, her bare feet pounding on the sand a few steps behind Ruby. Hildy's heart thudded like a wild drum in anticipation of the man's yelling, "Sic 'em, Tige!"

"Hey!" the male voice called again from behind them.

Ruby panted, "Don't look back! Jist keep a-runnin'!"

The voice called again, urgently. "Hildy! Ruby! Why are you running away?"

Hildy slowed and glanced over her shoulder. It was already too dark to see well, but she recognized that voice. She stopped and called, "Spud!"

"Who'd you think it was?" the boy asked, trotting toward the girls with his Airedale bounding along beside him.

Ruby slid to a stop. She turned to rage at the boy. "What'd ye mean, scaring us out of a year's growth?"

"Easy!" Hildy cautioned in a low voice, relieved but still shaky. "Don't start another argument with him."

Ruby's fear had obviously been turned to anger. She snapped, "Thar ye go a-stickin' up fer him ag'in!"

That remark and the edge to Ruby's tone rankled Hildy. But she bit her tongue and turned to face the boy. "What happened to you today? The truant officer catch you?"

Spud grinned at her. "No, but he sure is after me! I had a hard time giving him the slip. Then I knew he'd be watching for me to come back. So I hid out down here and watched the salmon. I was just thinking about heading over for your place when I heard your voices."

Ruby muttered, "When are ye a-goin' to Chicago?"

Hildy reached out and gave her cousin's arm a warning squeeze.

That made Ruby angry. "See ye back at yore place, Hildy," she said over her shoulder. "Alone!" She stalked off toward the bridge.

Spud asked, "What's the matter with her?"

"She'll be okay. Did you see Brother Ben?" Hildy asked hopefully.

"Yes, but I'm not planning to stay here, even if he does find somebody who could become my guardian. I'm my own man, and I'm going to stay that way."

Hildy tried a different approach. "A week from Saturday our homeroom is going on a field trip to see a dirigible land not far from San Francisco. I wish you could come along."

"I'll be near Chicago by then."

"You could stay here."

"And have the truant officer chasing me every day?"

"You could start school."

"Oh, sure! When they ask me to write down my address and my parents' names, I'll be hauled off as a truant!"

"Maybe you could stay with Brother Ben awhile longer. Everybody knows him. Maybe he'd let you put him down as your guardian for a little while, until we—uh, he finds somebody who'll do that permanently."

Hildy realized that she sounded a little desperate. She added lamely, "I mean, if you really want."

"I told you, Hildy—I'm hoboing to Chicago! I just stuck

around long enough to say goodbye!" His voice was sharp with reproach.

"Don't get upset! If—if you really want to go, then let's not quarrel. I don't want to remember you going off half mad."

The boy took a slow, deep breath. "Okay." He hesitated, then added, "You mentioned dirigibles. I've seen them land at the naval air station in Lakehurst, New Jersey. Other dirigibles land there too. Well, they don't land like an airplane, of course. They moor to a mast."

Hildy became excited. "Tell me about it! Maybe I could use some of what you've seen in my essay instead of just what I could get out of reading books."

"What do you want to know?"

"What does one of those dirigibles look like up close?"

"Well, they're longer than a battleship, and not easy to moor. When one comes in for a landing, it drops water that's been used as ballast. It's sort of like a miniature waterfall that lasts only a second.

"Since they're Navy dirigibles, they carry two or three tiny airplanes as scouts. They're called Curtiss F9C–2 Sparrowhawk biplanes. They're suspended on the underside of the dirigible by skyhooks. That's so the planes can scout around over the ocean, then land under the dirigible's trapeze. After that, the planes are lifted into a hangar inside the fuselage."

Hildy marveled, "You sure know a lot, Spud!"

He shrugged. "I like to read."

"Self-education's great, I guess, but people need regular education too. That's why I'm going to college someday, no matter how hard I have to work to do it."

Spud's tone changed. "You're not going to try getting me to go back to school again, are you?"

"Would it be so terrible?"

"It would if it means giving up my freedom." Spud's voice began to show anger. "I like being a hobo! I like going and coming as I please! I don't like being shut up in a classroom with a bunch of kids and a teacher!"

"Please don't get upset, Spud. If I didn't care—I mean, if a lot of us didn't care, I wouldn't say anything. But you've got a brain, and you know how to use it."

"I use it the way I want!" Spud snapped.

Hildy had to force herself to take a moment to think how to get off of this sensitive subject. She remembered what Brother Ben had said about having seen how each generation tended to follow the model of the one before.

"Did your father run away when he was a boy?"

Spud frowned. "Why do you ask?"

"Just a hunch. Did he?"

"Well, yes. When he was about thirteen, he got tired of his old man beating him, so he ran away to sea. Never saw his family again."

Hildy stopped and looked up at Spud. "So your grandfather beat your father, and he ran away?"

"So what?" Spud's voice was sharp again.

"Don't you see?" Hildy cried. "Unless something happens to break the cycle, you're probably going to grow up and be just like your father and his father before him."

"I'd never beat my kids, if I ever have any!" Spud said grimly.

"That's the only model you've got!" Hildy's concern made her voice rise. "Oh, it isn't that you intend to be like them, but unless you do something to change it, it's almost sure to happen!"

Spud's eyes narrowed in suspicion. "Those are mighty big thoughts for a twelve-year-old! Somebody been talking to you?"

Hildy started walking toward the bridge again. "Think about it," she suggested, then quickly changed the subject. "Too bad you can't be on that field trip to see the dirigibles."

"Well, I can't. So let's talk about something else."

"Okay. Do you want to know why Ruby and I ran from you awhile ago?" she asked. When he nodded, she explained about the tramp and his threats.

"You be careful," he said softly.

"I will be. I'm sure the Farnhams will be too." The thought of the stranger made Hildy uncomfortable. She didn't want to think about it anymore. She said, "Tell me more about dirigibles."

"They're incredible! Imagine seeing something the size of

two city blocks drifting high overhead, something ten stories tall and . . ."

"Oh!" Hildy interrupted, "Wish I had a pencil so I could write that down."

The boy smiled. "Then I'll save the rest until we get to your place."

Uncle Nate's topless Model T was parked outside the barn-house when Hildy and Spud approached.

Hildy opened the door. "Molly, Uncle Nate! I'm back—with Spud!"

Spud removed his aviator cap and followed her into the barn-house.

Nate Konning stood up from where he'd been sitting on an upended lug box. Hildy saw him do a double take at the sight of the ugly bruise on Spud's cheek, but Spud didn't seem to notice. Hildy glanced at her stepmother and realized that she had also seen the bruise. Molly shook her head sadly.

"Hi, Hildy. Spud, good to see you," Ruby's father said, shaking hands. "Ruby just walked in and said you were coming." He nodded toward his daughter who was playing in a back corner with Hildy's little sisters and the pet raccoon.

Molly asked, "Can all of you stay for supper?"

Nate shook his head. "Much obliged, Molly, but Ruby and I've got to be running along."

"Same here," Spud replied. "Thanks anyway, Mrs. Corrigan."

Nate urged, "Spud, ride along with Ruby and me. We'll give you a lift into town. Molly told me you're staying with Brother Ben."

Hildy saw her cousin walking toward her father. Ruby's face hardened in disapproval at the idea of Spud being in the same car with her.

Spud didn't seem to notice. "Thanks, no, Mr. Konning. Hildy wants me to tell her something about dirigibles for her essay, so I'll do that. Then I'll be on my way."

"Suit yourself," Nate answered, again shaking hands with the boy. "See all of you later."

Hildy found a stub of carpenter's pencil and a lined letter pad, while her little sisters gathered around the kitchen table, looking at Spud.

Elizabeth asked in innocent wonder, "How'd you hurt yourself?"

"Elizabeth!" Hildy said reprovingly, sitting down on the bench opposite Spud. "You know not to ask personal questions."

"It's okay," Spud said. He glanced at the younger sisters. "My old man—I mean, my father struck me."

Martha, the seven-year-old, said, "Our daddy sometimes spanks us, but he never leaves marks."

Hildy caught Spud's eye and realized he was probably thinking about what she'd said of children imitating their parents.

Spud's actions seemed to confirm Hildy's guess. He stood up, replacing his aviator cap on his head. "Well, I've got to be going," he said.

Hildy wanted to remind him that he'd promised to tell her more about dirigibles, but she didn't say anything. Spud went out into the dark with his dog Lindy beside him.

Hildy stared silently after him, wondering if she would ever see him again. The thought made her very sad.

Hildy's father arrived shortly after that. He gathered the family around the kitchen table and explained, "The foreman let four riders go today."

Elizabeth leaned close to Hildy and whispered, "We're moving again, so there goes your scholarship!"

Her father gave Elizabeth a hard look, making her squirm and lower her eyes. Then he continued. "I'm one of those he kept on."

Molly let out a little glad cry and reached over to kiss him on his black-stubbled cheek.

"That's only part of it," he added. "I saw our landlord at the little store where I stopped to pick up some razor blades. He wants this barn-house back."

Hildy reminded him, "Some time ago, you told us that we'd have to move. It'll be too hard to heat this place in winter."

Her father nodded, slamming his work-hardened open palm down on the table so hard the lamp jumped. "Yes, but it aggravates the stuffing out of me that we've only got to the end of the month to do it!"

Elizabeth slid off the bench and ran to the drugstore calendar that hung on the wall by the kitchen range. "Today's the 19th so that leaves . . ." her voice dropped as she counted, then it rose again. "Twelve days to the 30th. That's a Sunday!"

Her father nodded. "I know, and I don't get paid until the first. So that means we'll have no money for rent even if I can find a place where they'll take kids; much less a raccoon." He glanced meaningfully at Hildy.

Elizabeth asked, "Then when will we move?"

"Maybe I can get the new landlord to trust me for one day. If so, we'll move on Sunday, because that's the only day I have off. Hildy, you and your sisters will have to help Molly have everything packed by the 29th."

"But, Daddy, that's the day of the dirigible field trip! I've got to go in order to write a better essay for the scholarship!"

"Can't help it, Hildy," her father replied.

Hildy nodded, numb with the realization that he was right. She took a quick breath and asked a question, dreading the answer. "Where do you think we'll move?"

"Well, since I still have my job, you can forget about Grass Valley. On Sunday, when I don't have to work, I'll see if I can find a house around here."

Hildy let out a long, slow sigh of relief. "You'll try to get a place where I can still go to the same school, won't you? I don't want to lose out on that scholarship."

"I'm not making any promises," her father said. "I've got to do the best I can, and if that means I can't find a house around here, then we'll just have to move to another town, maybe even out of state."

"But my scholarship!" Hildy cried. "I need . . ."

"I know what you need!" her father exclaimed. "But all of us need a roof over our heads now!" His tone softened. He reached out and took Hildy's hand. "I know how much that scholarship means to you, so I'll do my best to find a place where you won't have to change schools."

Hildy impulsively hugged him. "Thank you, Daddy!"

As she said her prayers later that night, Hildy included concern for Spud, safety for the Farnhams, wisdom to deal with the problems at school, and a right decision for Ruby's father. She hoped he wouldn't move back to the Ozarks with Ruby.

Finally Hildy whispered an urgent petition from her pallet in the pitch blackness of the barn-house. "Please let Daddy find us a house where I don't have to change schools and lose out on trying to win that hundred dollars. I need it so much for my college fund!"

———

The next morning Hildy and Ruby arrived at their homeroom shortly after the first bell rang. Only Edna and Tessie were already seated when Hildy and Ruby slid into their desks.

Miss Krutz walked down to Hildy as Zelpha and other students began coming into the room. Hildy looked up a little anxiously as Miss Krutz stopped at her desk. Zelpha had to stop behind her.

The teacher said, "Hildy, I've been looking at your transfer records. In spite of the fact you've moved many times to different states, you've achieved remarkable academic standards."

Hildy was surprised because her teacher's tone was less formal than usual when directed at her. Hildy nodded but said nothing. She glanced around nervously, unsure of why Miss Krutz was saying this.

Hildy glimpsed Zelpha standing behind the teacher. There was something in Zelpha's eyes Hildy had never seen before.

Miss Krutz added briskly, "I shall look forward to seeing what you can do in this school, Hildy."

"Yes ma'm," Hildy said softly.

The teacher walked on down to the end of the aisle, allowing Zelpha to sit down behind Hildy just as the second bell rang.

Miss Krutz raised her voice for the rest of the class. "Tomorrow Mr. Stanway, the local Studebaker dealer, will be our guest at this time. He'll tell us something about his own background and why he gives a scholarship to a seventh grader each year. I'm sure he'll be an inspiration to us all. Hopefully, each of you will want to try harder to be the one in this room chosen to receive the award."

Hildy closed her eyes momentarily. *Lord,* she prayed silently, *let me be that one!*

The teacher turned to the blackboard. "Today we'll begin learning about the origin and history of dirigibles to help you write your essays."

Hildy felt a light tap on her shoulder. She half turned her head. Zelpha slipped her a piece of paper. Hildy glanced down at the printed words.

You can't win. I'll see to that.

It was unsigned. Hildy twisted around to return the paper to Zelpha.

Miss Krutz snapped, "Hildy, bring that to me!"

Reluctantly, Hildy stood up and did as she was told. Miss Krutz glanced at the note, then scowled at Hildy. "I'm deeply disappointed in you—threatening instead of trying to compete honestly!"

Hildy blinked in surprise. "I didn't write . . ."

"Don't compound your error, Hildy! Return to your seat. But I'll keep this as a black mark against you."

Miss Krutz opened her desk drawer and dropped the paper inside. Hildy returned to her seat, head down, cheeks searing with embarrassment at the unfairness of what had happened.

By the time the bell rang, ending the period, Hildy had made up her mind about one thing. She hurried out of her seat behind Ruby. Hildy wanted to be in the hallway before Zelpha and her friends got there.

Ruby asked hotly, "Why didn't ye tell her who writ that note?"

Hildy watched the homeroom door as other students filed out. She said, "You know she wouldn't have believed me. Besides, I hoped she'd recognize her own niece's handwriting. But it was printed, so maybe she didn't."

"Or maybe she did and let on she didn't!" Ruby's voice rose. "If'n it was me, I'd snatch that Zelpha baldheaded! An' I'd tell Miss Krutz a thing or two besides!"

Hildy saw Zelpha leaving the room with her two friends and walked up to them. "Zelpha, I want to talk to you," Hildy said. "Your friends can go on ahead."

Ruby snapped, "Ye two done heerd her! Move!"

When Hildy and Zelpha were alone, Hildy said earnestly, "I have nothing against you, so why are you trying to get me in trouble?"

Zelpha asked, "What does it matter to you?" She glanced scathingly at Hildy's handmade clothes.

Hildy replied with passion, "That's just the reason I need to win that scholarship! I want to change my life! And I want to help a lot of other people make their lives better too. I've got a plan to do that."

"I don't care what you've got planned." Zelpha sneered. She started to walk away.

Hildy stepped in front of her. "I don't know why you hate me. I'm just doing my best to win. I hope you'll do your best too. If you win fairly, I'll be happy for you. But I won't be scared off. So, in the meantime, can't we be friends?"

The strange look returned to Zelpha's eyes, the same one Hildy had seen awhile ago. For a moment, Zelpha's mouth worked, but no words came. When they did, her tone had changed.

"You don't understand! I have to win! I have no choice!" Zelpha voice rose. "I'll do anything to win! Anything!"

Zelpha broke away and ran down the hallway, leaving Hildy surprised and confused, with a new sense of danger.

CHAPTER
TEN

—

MORE BAD NEWS

Wednesday

Hildy caught up to Ruby in the hallway and related her conversation with Zelpha.

Ruby asked, "What do ye reckon she meant?"

"I can't imagine. But she sounded so—I don't know—sort of desperate."

Ruby snorted. "What's she got to be desprit about? Her daddy's president of the trustees and so big in this school that if he says 'Jump!' ever'body asks 'How high?' and does it."

"I wish I knew more about him."

"Zelpha's father? What on earth fer?"

"Well, Brother Ben told me that when Miss Krutz was younger, her brother didn't like any of her boyfriends and ran them all off."

"So?" Ruby challenged.

"So maybe Miss Krutz isn't as mean as I first thought. Like all those nice things she said about me today." Hildy stopped walking and looked at her cousin. "She didn't know Zelpha was behind her, but I saw a funny look come into Zelpha's eyes."

"What kinda look?"

"I'm not sure. Surprised, I guess. Then she really acted

strange—sort of frantic—when I talked to her in the hallway."

The cousins entered their next class just as the final bell rang, and they didn't get a chance to talk again until lunch. Hildy was still deep in thought about the morning's events, trying unsuccessfully to understand what Zelpha had meant.

Both girls had brought money they had earned themselves. So at noon, the cousins started to walk the two short blocks to the dime store in downtown Lone River to buy the necessary three-hole binder, pen and other supplies they would need in various classes.

Hildy and Ruby had just crossed the street with their lunch pails when Hildy stopped. "Whoops! I forgot my orange. It wouldn't fit inside my pail. Wait here. I'll be right back."

Hildy was eager to enjoy the orange. Because two dozen oranges cost twenty-one cents, they were a rare treat.

The hallways were totally deserted, so Hildy quickly reached the cloakroom in back of her homeroom. Just as she reached for the orange on the shelf above the coat hooks, she heard a drawer opening.

Sounds like Miss Krutz's back at her desk, Hildy thought. *I don't want to see her just now. She might bawl me out some more for writing that note.*

Hildy delayed, staying silently in the cloakroom until she heard the desk drawer close. A moment later, when the outside classroom door gently closed, Hildy took her orange and made her way to the hallway.

It was still silent and empty. *That's strange!* Hildy told herself. *How did Miss Krutz disappear so fast?*

Ruby was standing across the street from the school eating a mashed-potato sandwich when Hildy rejoined her. At the same moment, Ben Strong's bright yellow two-door Packard pulled to the curb in front of the girls. Hildy was happy to see that Spud was with him.

Ruby muttered, "I shore wish Spud would leave town!"

"Shh!" Hildy said under her breath. "You go on. I'll meet you in the dime store in a few minutes."

Ruby nodded and walked away, licking her fingers of mashed potatoes that had oozed out of the sandwich.

Hildy took a couple of quick steps to the curb and bent her head to look inside the car. "Hi!" she said brightly. "What brings you two. . .?" her voice trailed off at the sight of their somber faces. "What's wrong?" she cried in sudden alarm.

Spud said softly, "Connie's disappeared."

"What?" The word exploded from Hildy's mouth.

"It's true," the old Ranger said, giving his handlebar moustache a flip with the back of his right forefinger. "Matt Farnham just called me. He said Dickie was at school. Connie was taking a nap, but when she seemed to sleep longer than usual, her mother checked, and the girl was gone. They think she wandered outside."

"The river!" Hildy gasped. "Oh, no!"

Spud said quietly, "Mr. Farnham asked Ben if he'd help look, so I'm going along."

"Me too!" Hildy cried, reaching for the door handle. "Scoot over, Spud!"

Ben said, "Hold on, Hildy! You can't leave school without permission."

"That's right!" Hildy's mind spun, thinking of the little four-year-old rolling down the bluff behind the mansion and into the river. "But there's no time to ask the principal."

Ben insisted, "You can't risk getting expelled for breaking the rules! I know the principal, so I'll go explain to him. But you'd better run tell your homeroom teacher."

In her concern for Connie, Hildy didn't think about running after Ruby to tell her the news. Instead, Hildy dashed across the street, into the school building and down the still empty hallway with a prayer on her lips. *Don't let her drown! And let Miss Krutz be in her room!*

Hildy jerked the door open hard, relieved to see the teacher. "Miss Krutz! Miss Krutz!" Hildy panted, running to the desk and setting her lunch pail down. "The little girl I take . . ."

"I'm surprised at you, Hildy!" the teacher broke in, her eyes hard. "How could you?"

Hildy recoiled in surprise. "What?"

"Don't deny it and make things worse!"

"Make what worse?" Hildy asked in confusion.

The teacher pointed to her open desk drawer. "Taking the note so there'd be no evidence against you."

Hildy's eyes opened wide. "I didn't!"

"I saw you, Hildy Corrigan!" The teacher's voice cracked like a buggy whip. "I was standing just inside Mrs. Blackman's door across the way, talking to her awhile ago, when I saw you leave this room!"

"I forgot my orange and came back for it. But I didn't go near your . . . Wait, I remember something! While I was in the cloak-room, I heard your desk drawer open. But I thought it was you."

"Then why didn't you come out and speak to me?"

"I—I didn't want to see you just then."

"I'll say you didn't! You didn't want anyone to see you! You'd have succeeded except that I happened to be across the hall with Mrs. Blackman. Hildy, I am terribly disappointed in you. That's another black mark . . ."

"But I didn't . . . Oh, I can't talk now! I've got to go!" Hildy turned and dashed across the room.

"Come back here!"

"I can't!" Hildy cried from the door, anguish in her voice. "I'll tell you why later!"

"You go out that door, and you can forget the Studebaker scholar . . ."

Hildy didn't hear the rest because the door slammed shut behind her. But she could guess, and she moaned.

Sick at heart, Hildy returned to the Packard just as Brother Ben slid back under the wheel. Hildy squeezed past Spud and plopped down in the leather backseat, panting hard. Her mind spun wildly with the two totally unexpected events of the last few minutes.

Ben looked at her in the rearview mirror. "You look sick," he said. "You going to be all right?"

Hildy took a deep breath and almost blurted out what had happened with Miss Krutz. Slowly, her mind racing, Hildy let her breath out and made a decision. She forced herself to put aside the misunderstanding with Miss Krutz and concentrate on the most important thing.

She urged, "Please don't worry about me. Drive faster! And tell me about Connie."

Spud twisted in the front seat to look back at her with concerned eyes. "I was there when Ben got the call, so you know as much as we do."

Ben added, "They thought my tracking experience might be helpful, but it's been a long time. I'll do what I can, of course."

Hildy had a sudden mental image of the little girl's straight blonde hair floating on the river below her parents' home. "Lord, no!" Hildy whispered. It was a prayer of agony torn from Hildy's aching heart.

Suddenly, she stiffened. "The tramp!" she exclaimed, leaning forward. She quickly told Ben about the stranger's shouted threat to Mrs. Farnham.

As the car continued into the country, Hildy, Spud, and the old Ranger discussed the possibility that the tramp had kidnapped Connie. Hildy asked Spud if he'd seen any tracks of a man and a big dog when he was at the river. Spud said he hadn't, but he hadn't been near the bend in the river that Hildy had described.

Ben tried to sound reassuring. "Since the Lindbergh kidnapping law went into effect, I doubt anyone would risk the death penalty by abducting a child. It's more likely she wandered away and got lost. We'll find her."

Hildy wasn't sure if Ben really believed that or if he was trying to keep her hopes up. Yet it was obvious that a new and threatening possibility existed, because the rest of the trip was made in fearful silence.

Soon the big Packard left the county road and turned onto the long paved lane lined with old elm and sycamore trees leading to the Farnham home. Beyond the open gate, the gray-painted Victorian mansion stood majestically in the center of three acres of shade trees. The trees, along with the roses that grew everywhere, made the grounds look like a park. Several cars were parked haphazardly on the lawn around the northern carriage entrance.

"Sheriff's here," Ben said, looking toward a Model A Ford with a golden insignia on the front door.

Still in silence, the three climbed out of the Packard. Hildy followed Ben and Spud up the few wooden stairs to the screened-in porch that ran the entire length of the house.

"Where's everybody?" Hildy asked in a hushed voice as she followed Ben and Spud across the porch to the dark walnut door with a frosted-glass window.

"Probably down at the river," Ben replied, taking off his cowboy hat. He added, "Except Beryl—I mean, Mrs. Farnham." He twisted the handle in the middle of the walnut door.

The bell had barely sounded somewhere deep inside the mansion when an older woman opened the door. Behind her, Hildy saw several other women standing silently in the hallway. These were obviously neighbors who had come to be with the distraught mother.

Mrs. Farnham, in her wheelchair, rolled herself up beside the older woman who'd opened the door.

"Oh, Ben!" Mrs. Farnham exclaimed, reaching out to grip the old Ranger's hand. "Hildy! Spud! Thank you for coming! I feel so helpless in this wheelchair. I can't even look for my own child."

"We'll do it for you, Beryl," Ben replied.

"Everyone's at the river looking for her," Mrs. Farnham said.

Ben nodded. "We'll go right down and help."

Hildy added, "Don't worry, Mrs. Farnham."

Spud asked, "Can you tell us how it happened? When did you last see Connie? Where?"

Ben said in his quiet, soft drawl, "They'll tell us down at the river." He replaced his hat and turned away.

Hildy and Spud started to follow, but Mrs. Farnham spoke again. "Hildy, Dickie's so upset he's run upstairs and won't come down! None of us can comfort him. Would you. . .?"

"Yes, ma'm," Hildy replied. She would have preferred to help search for Connie and learn more details of her disappearance, but taking care of the six-year-old boy was more important right now.

When the matronly woman stepped back, Hildy waved to Ben and Spud, then entered the door. She gave Mrs. Farnham a quick pat on the shoulder and hurried inside.

Hildy nodded to the silent women as she hastened across the rich Persian rug and up the stairs. Hildy found the boy sprawled face down across the bed that once had been his. He looked up with tear-stained face as the girl entered.

"Did they find Connie?" he asked.

Hildy sat down beside him. "No, but they will." She began stroking the boy's curly golden hair.

He snuggled closer, putting his head on Hildy's lap. "When I got home from school, Mommy said Connie was gone. She's scared 'cause maybe Connie fell in the river."

Hildy put her arms around the boy and pulled him close so her cheek was against the top of his head. "I'm sure she'll be all right, so you mustn't worry."

"Could we go help look for her?"

"Let's ask your mother if that's okay."

Downstairs, Mrs. Farnham gave her approval, but warned Hildy and Dickie to stay on the grounds, well away from the river. "Don't let Dickie out of your sight," Mrs. Farnham warned.

"I'll be careful," Hildy said.

She took the little boy's hand, led him into the large, old-fashioned kitchen and onto the smaller screened-in back porch. Hildy's mind leaped momentarily back to the encounter with her teacher, but she shook it off and tried to think where Connie might be.

Hildy unhooked the simple latch and pushed the screen door open for Dickie. A piece of paper between the door and the jamb fluttered into the rosebush growing beside the three back steps.

"What's that?" Dickie asked, descending the steps.

"Don't know," Hildy answered. She gingerly reached past a thick cluster of fragrant red floribunda roses and retrieved the folded piece of common butcher paper. Hildy took the three steps to the path before opening the paper. Walking behind Dickie, she glanced down.

Hildy stopped in disbelief as the first words on the page hit her with the force of a blow.

I have the kid. Don't call the G-men, or you'll never see her again.

—

CHAPTER ELEVEN

DEADLINE IN THREE DAYS

Wednesday Afternoon

M oments later, Mrs. Farnham read the ransom note and shrieked, "Lord, no!" The paper slipped from her trembling fingers.

Dickie wriggled free of Hildy's arms and threw himself across one wheel of his mother's chair. "Mommy, Mommy! What's the matter?"

Mrs. Farnham cried and hugged the boy tightly while a neighbor woman picked up the fallen paper. Hildy pushed into the circle of other women who strained to read the note. The girl skimmed the chilling part she'd already read and finished the rest:

> Put $10,000 in $20 bills into a plain paper sack. More instructions will come to your home phone. Everything must be completed by noon this Sunday, or your daughter will never come home again.

Hildy turned to look at Mrs. Farnham. "You think it was the tramp who threatened you and chased Ruby and me?"

"I don't know what to think! My husband . . ."

"I'll get him!" Hildy interrupted. She whirled to look at the nearest neighbor woman. "Watch Dickie, please!" She jerked her head toward the boy, then rushed outside.

She found Ben and Spud searching along the river near the bluff in back of the Farnham property. She blurted out the news about the note.

As she finished, Mr. Farnham and a man in a deputy sheriff's khaki uniform emerged from some willows. Hildy sprinted to them and gasped out her story.

When the two started running toward the bluff, Hildy started to follow, then turned to face the eighty-five-year-old Ben.

"You and Spud go on. I'll be there soon," the old Ranger said.

Hildy hesitated, then shook her head. "I'll go with you," she said, falling into step beside him. Fallen acorns crunched under their feet.

Spud joined them. "Tell us again exactly what you remember about the note."

Hurrying toward the bluff at the bank of the Farnham property, Hildy recalled every detail possible.

When she had finished, the old Ranger nodded thoughtfully. "It's strange that he'd set a deadline three and a half days away. I'd expect he would have wanted to get it all done as soon as possible, within twenty-four hours, at least."

"Noon Sunday," Spud mused. "Ben, do you think there's a clue in the note that you could use to help us find Connie before then?"

"Right now, all we've got is the note. Not much help there. Butcher paper's common. Comes in long pinkish roles from the butcher shop and the grocery store. Clipping words from a newspaper to make the message means there's no handwriting. I'll have to see the note, but from what Hildy said, I'd guess the letters were probably stuck on with plain old flour-and-water paste."

Hildy asked, "So there are no clues in the note?"

"I can't be sure until I examine it," Ben answered. He was breathing a little hard from the brisk pace. He glanced up at the bluff marking the back end of the Farnham's property.

Spud started climbing the narrow ledge in the face of the bluff, but Hildy noticed that the old Ranger seemed to be having a little difficulty getting his breath. She stopped, saying, "I need to rest a minute."

Spud turned around, caught her eye and realized why she was stopping. "Me too," he said.

The three stood in silence a moment, their breathing loud in the still, September afternoon air.

Hildy asked anxiously, "Isn't there something we can do to get Connie back before those three days are up?"

"That'll depend on what Matt decides about calling in the Federal Bureau of Investigation against the kidnapper's warning," Ben said. "But no matter what he decides, I can quietly try to learn if food, blankets, or such things have been stolen from neighbors."

The old Ranger again started up the steep bluff. He continued, "I can follow up on those things as possible clues. However, I can't think of anything you and Spud can do, except pray and try to help the Farnhams."

Hildy followed Ben up the path. Spud trailed behind and said, "I can't figure why anybody would be foolish enough to risk kidnapping, not after the Lindbergh case."

The whole country knew about the aviator's terrible ordeal two years ago. Spud's hero, the man who'd flown the Atlantic alone in a single-engine monoplane, was still grieving with his wife, Anne Morrow Lindbergh, about the kidnap-murder of their young son. A death penalty for kidnappers had resulted.

Hildy said, "In this case, we at least know what the man looks like who took Connie."

"You and Ruby do," Spud reminded her. "And Mrs. Farnham and her son, maybe her husband too. But Ben and I never saw him."

Ben said, "Whoa there, you two! Just because the tramp chased you girls and threatened the Farnhams doesn't necessarily mean he's the kidnapper."

"I'm sure it's the same man!" Hildy swiveled her head to look toward the river. "Do you suppose he's hiding out down here somewhere? Maybe he's got Connie real close by."

The old Ranger stopped on the trail, puffing from the climb. "Spud and I saw tracks along the sandbars."

"What kind of tracks?" Hildy asked anxiously. "A man's and a big dog's?"

"Yes," Ben admitted, "but then we weren't looking for a kidnapper. We were looking for the little lost girl."

Spud added sadly, "The deputy told us to look in the water. That's where he really expected to find her."

Ben cleared his throat. "But now we know she didn't drown, or even wander off by herself."

Hildy said with alarm, "Maybe we should go right down there and try to find her!"

"Easy, Hildy!" the old Ranger said. "We can't do anything until we learn what Matt decides to do."

Hildy took a slow, deep breath and studied the river. It snaked close to the bottom of the bluff behind the Farnham's property, then twisted away to the left to make a big S curve. In the distance, past the oaks on the bottom land, the river turned right.

Hildy couldn't see the big bend where she and Ruby had been chased by the man and his dog. That was near a small white cliff. However, above that, on the flat farmland, she saw acres of eight-feet-high corn still standing in neat brown rows. To her right, Hildy could see the trees marking the river's path toward a bridge and the graveled county road.

Hildy said thoughtfully, "I keep thinking there was something about that man who chased us—something important. But I can't think what it is."

"If that stranger who chased you girls is the same one who kidnapped Connie," Spud said, "he's probably not down there on the river anymore. If he had been, and any of us who were searching for Connie had come close, his dog would have barked at us. But we didn't hear any barking, not even at the neighbor men who joined the search."

"Maybe the dog is guarding Connie," Hildy suggested, "and he's trained not to bark."

"He barked at you and Ruby, didn't he?" Spud asked. When Hildy nodded, he added, "I think he'd have barked if we came close too. So he's probably not still down there, and neither is Connie."

"No use standing here guessing," Ben said. "Let's get back to the house and see if we can put all the pieces of this puzzle together to find that little girl."

At the mansion Mr. Farnham told Hildy that he and his wife were going to stay by the telephone, awaiting the kidnapper's call. Ben would stay with them, but Hildy was asked to take Dickie outside and keep him busy.

At the barn she persuaded the little boy to curry the old mare. Hildy perched thoughtfully on a bale of hay and watched the boy.

I wish there was something I could do to help find Connie!

Hildy's thoughts jumped, recalling the awful encounter with Miss Krutz over the missing note. *She'll count that as two black marks against me! One for writing it and one for stealing it. No, she'll make it three, because I ran away. Maybe Mr. Wiley will tell her what Brother Ben told him, and Miss Krutz won't count the last thing.*

Hildy sighed heavily, feeling the weight of so many things pressing down on her. *But I can't quit! I just can't, because I need that scholarship so much.* She shook her head. *Right now, getting Connie back safely is the most important thing. But how—with only three and a half days left?*

Hildy stood up and crossed to the window opening and gazed moodily past the bluff toward the river. *What is it that I'm overlooking down there?* she wondered.

She turned at the sound of the barn door opening. Spud and Lindy stood there. Spud motioned for Hildy to come. She told Dickie she'd be right back and asked him to keep brushing the horse.

Hildy followed Spud outside into the late afternoon sunlight. She turned so she could face Spud and still see the little boy inside the barn.

"What is it?" Hildy asked.

"Mr. Farnham's decided to follow the kidnapper's instructions. They won't call in the Federal Bureau of Investigation—the G-men—but wait for the kidnapper to contact them. They'll have the money ready too."

"Do they think that's wise?"

"The deputy says it's a mistake, but Mr. Farnham is adamant about it. He also doesn't want any one of us to talk about this. We need to keep it to ourselves."

Hildy thought of the neighbor women in the house who knew about the kidnapping, and of all their husbands still hunting in the river bottom. They'd all know.

She asked, "Do you think that's possible?"

"It's a small town, so everybody'll probably hear that Connie's missing. The search will continue for the sake of appearance, but without the authorities, especially the G-men. Since it's the Farnhams' daughter who's life is at risk, all of us who know the truth have agreed to abide by the Farnhams' wishes—with two exceptions."

"You mean Ruby and me?"

Spud nodded. "Because you and Ruby saw the man, and he chased you, Ben says you two should tell your parents. We don't want to scare them or you, but Ben says it's possible that you two might be in some—danger."

Hildy shook her head in bewilderment. "If we stay out of the river bottom, why would he bother us?"

"Because you're possible witnesses."

Hildy's mouth suddenly went dry with fear. "You mean because we would be able to identify him?"

Spud nodded. "It's not likely he would do anything, Ben says, but it's something to keep in mind."

"Mrs. Farnham and Dickie also saw the tramp—twice, in fact!"

"The deputy said he could arrange for plainclothes police to keep an eye on them from a distance. Mr. Farnham doesn't want anything to look unusual, in case the kidnapper might be watching this place."

Ben came striding up. He looked somber. "Hildy," he began in his soft voice, "I guess Spud's told you everything so far."

"Yes, except how Connie was kidnapped."

"Mrs. Farnham says Connie was taking a nap in her downstairs bedroom on the south side of the house. Beryl and her daughter were the only ones in the house. Mrs. Farnham was working on her household budget on the kitchen table. She checked on Connie once, and she was fine. But when Connie didn't wake up at her usual time, Beryl rolled her chair in to check. Connie was gone."

Hildy asked, "Did Mrs. Farnham hear or see anything?"

"No," Ben replied. "Not a thing."

Spud joined in. "At first, she didn't think about the tramp and his threats. She just thought Connie had gotten up and wandered outside."

"Oh!" Hildy said, hurting inside for the Farnhams, and especially for the little four-year-old.

Ben said, "There's one thing more, Hildy. Spud and I told the Farnhams about the man and his dog chasing you and Ruby last Sunday. Matt and the deputy both think it's highly unlikely that the man is still down there or that he has Connie hidden somewhere close by. But," he added, "if he is down there, he won't know that his note wasn't found until after all those men were down by the river looking for Connie."

A frightened thought leaped into Hildy's mind. She asked fearfully, "You mean he might have seen them, and he might think the FBI's been called in?"

Ben shook his head. "No, because those searchers were obviously ranchers, neighbors—except for the deputy in uniform. Anyway, let's pray Connie's not in any more danger than before."

Hildy said fervently, "I just keep having this strangest feeling . . ."

Ben interrupted. "Mr. Farnham's going back down there tonight with the deputy to have another look for the tramp—or some sign of him or Connie."

Hildy frowned. "But if he's really down there, won't he see the lanterns or flashlights?"

"In case they're spotted, both Matt and the deputy—in plain clothes—will carry spears as though they're after salmon. It should be safe."

Spud snapped his fingers. "Hey! If that doesn't work, tomorrow I could take Lindy and go down there. If the guy's watching, he'll think it's just a kid with a dog. Maybe I could find some sign or something."

Ben said, "Too bad an Airedale can't trail a person the way a bloodhound can."

"Yeah," Spud said glumly. "Lindy's a great dog, but he's just that. He's not a trail hound. Yet he sure is a terror if he thinks somebody's threatening me. He proved that a couple of times in hobo jungles."

Hildy looked at Dickie, who was still currying the horse, then turned to Spud again. She asked anxiously, "You won't leave for Chicago until this is over, will you?"

"I'll stay until then."

Hildy breathed a sigh of relief.

Ben said, "I talked it over with Matt and Beryl, and they're agreed it would be a good idea for someone to stay with them for a while. They'd like you to do that, Spud."

"Me?" Spud considered the thought a moment, then nodded. "Why not? I could go up and down stairs or anything they need. I could sleep in Dickie's room too."

Ben seemed satisfied. "Then I guess we all know what to do—act natural, keep alert, and wait for the kidnapper to call." He paused, then added, "Hildy, you and Ruby be extra careful. Remember, as witnesses, you may both be in danger."

A sudden lump of fear formed in Hildy's throat. She gulped, nodded, and glanced toward the river. "Connie's *really* in danger!" she said softly. "We've got to help find her—and fast! But how?"

CHAPTER
TWELVE

—

HARD CHOICES

Wednesday Evening, Thursday Morning

Darkness had settled when Ben, the old Texas Ranger, dropped Hildy off at the barn-house. Ruby and Molly rushed out, followed by Hildy's four little sisters.

Ruby asked sharply, "What happened to ye today? Last I seen, ye was a-startin' to talk to Brother Ben and Spud. Y'all tol' me to go on to the store and wait. Then ye never showed up, not even for afternoon classes!"

Molly, balancing the baby on her left hip, added, "You've had us worried half to death!"

"I'm sorry," Hildy said. "So many things happened . . ." She stopped, glancing at her four little sisters. Their eyes showed they'd also shared in the concern. Hildy knelt and motioned for them to all come close. She encircled them in her arms.

"I need to talk to Molly and Ruby alone. Elizabeth, would you take everyone inside and play for a while?"

When the reluctant little sisters had gone, Hildy told her stepmother and cousin all that had happened from the time she left Ruby until she came home.

Molly said softly, "Poor little Connie! She must be scared to death, wherever she is. And that awful man—does Ben think you and Ruby *really* might be in danger?"

"I don't want to think so, but we *can* identify the tramp. Maybe he doesn't want to risk letting that happen. Especially with kidnapping carrying a death penalty."

"I ain't skeered o' no tramp!" Ruby blustered.

Hildy smiled wanly. "Well, when you and I were running from him down by the river, I was scared."

"I was jist a-runnin' from his big ol' dawg."

"Just the same," Molly said, "You girls be careful! I'll be glad when we move. I just hope it isn't away from Northside School. Hildy, I want you to win that scholarship."

Hildy said, "I've hardly thought about the scholarship since Connie turned up missing."

Ruby grumbled, "I'm shore sorry, Hildy, but after Miss Krutz done decided ye stole that note from her desk, and ye run off when she was a-talkin' to ye about it, sounds like ye kin fergit that hunnert dollars!"

Hildy closed her eyes and nodded in painful thought.

Molly said firmly, "Look, Hildy. Life hands all of us some hard problems now and then, problems that stand between us and our goals. Lots of folks quit. But others don't. They're de-layed, but they never loose sight of their goal or their determi-nation to reach it. You're that kind of person, Hildy! Right now, finding Connie's important, but don't stop trying to win that scholarship, no matter how hard things seem."

Brother Ben's quotation about Paul the Apostle flashed in Hildy's mind. "This one thing I do . . . I press toward the mark . . ." Hildy's thoughts leaped. *Faith—and it grows strong by meeting resistance.*

Hildy's father wasn't home by suppertime, so Molly fed the kids and kept her husband's food warm on the back of the wood-burning range. Then Hildy helped her stepmother make the necessary pen wipers for school.

They had just finished when Joe Corrigan arrived, tired and cranky. He washed up, sat down in glum silence, and began eating. Hildy sensed it wasn't a good time to talk about the day's events.

At last he finished wiping gravy from his plate with a piece of biscuit. He leaned back and announced, "I was late because I heard about a place for rent. I went there after work. It's in the country a-ways."

Hildy felt her stomach lurch. "How far out?"

"Far enough out so you can keep your coon."

"What about school?" Hildy asked.

"One room. All grades."

Hildy turned away, stifling a groan of disappointment. Still, she didn't want to give up hope.

"Is it all set?" she asked.

"No. Be a few days before I know." He looked at his wife, daughter, and niece. "I can tell from looking at you three that something's happened. What is it?"

When Hildy had told him about the kidnapping and the old tramp, her father reached out and pulled her close. "I don't think there's anything to worry about, but any man who'd kidnap a little child might be desperate enough to do something else. You girls be careful. Stay close together when you can, and don't go anywhere that's risky."

Hildy glanced at her cousin, then back to her father. "I keep having this feeling that when we were chased, it had something to do with Connie's kidnapping. So I'd like to go back down . . ."

"No!" Her father released Hildy and looked at her sternly. "Absolutely not, young lady!"

"But if Connie's down there . . ."

"Let the grown-ups handle it!"

"Ruby and I could go together."

"No, I said!" Her father added firmly, "You cannot go down there, Hildy. Not even with Ruby."

———

The next morning Hildy managed to be first off the bus. She'd already explained her purpose to Ruby, so Hildy dashed across the school yard, up the stairs, and down the nearly empty hallways to her homeroom. She was relieved to see that her teacher was alone.

"Miss Krutz," Hildy began, approaching with her lunch bucket, "may I talk to you?"

"Of course." The teacher sat down on her chair and motioned Hildy to a desk in front of her. Miss Krutz continued, "After the rude way you behaved yesterday, I had no choice but to tell Mr. Wiley that I felt you should be disqualified from the scholarship competition."

Hildy's mouth dropped open. "Disqualified?"

"That was before Mr. Wiley told me about Ben Strong's visit to his office. I should have guessed when you rushed out of here yesterday that you had a very valid reason." Her tone softened. "I trust the Farnhams found their little girl?"

"Not yet," Hildy said, "but I'm sure they will."

Miss Krutz's voice showed genuine concern. "Because I didn't hear anything about it on the local radio station this morning, I assumed she'd been located."

Hildy was anxious to get off that subject because she didn't want to mention the kidnapping. She asked hopefully, "Then I'm still eligible for the scholarship?"

"You haven't explained why you took that note from my desk."

"I didn't take it. In fact, I didn't write it."

"Then who did?"

Hildy hesitated. "I—I can't tell you."

"Can't? Or won't?"

"Please—I just can't say who wrote it. And I don't know who took it."

Miss Krutz thoughtfully studied Hildy before saying anything. "I see." She stood up, walked around her desk and lightly touched the girl's shoulder.

Hildy was surprised at that.

The teacher turned and walked back to her desk. She said, "In answer to your question—yes, you're still qualified for the scholarship, and the field trip to see the dirigible."

"Thanks! Thanks a lot!"

A tiny smile showed on Miss Krutz's lips. "As I said before, Hildy, I've studied your transfer records. You've not only been a good academic student, but your lifelong deportment has been exemplary. I now understand about yesterday.

"However, I don't understand how you got in trouble that first day and ended up in the principal's office.

For a moment Hildy wanted to blurt out the whole truth. Then she remembered the teacher's relationship to Zelpha. Hildy looked directly into Miss Krutz's eyes and asked quietly, "Can't you?"

The teacher seemed to flinch. "Whatever do you mean, Hildy?" she demanded sharply.

"I can't say anything more—except I'm innocent of everything."

The first bell rang. Students started entering the class, ending Hildy's and Miss Krutz's discussion. Hildy headed for her desk.

Zelpha walked down the aisle with a hint of a frown on her face. She seemed to look at Hildy with a question in her eyes. Hildy was sure Zelpha knew she had been talking privately with their teacher. Hildy also guessed that Zelpha suspected Miss Krutz had been told the truth about the note, maybe about who started the scuffle the first day of school.

Now what will she do? Hildy asked herself.

The final bell rang, and the roll was taken. Miss Krutz asked how many had purchased their supplies. Everyone except Hildy had done so.

"Good!" the teacher said. "Hildy, make your purchase at noon. By tomorrow, all of you should bring your pen wipers to school.

"Now, while waiting for our guest to arrive, we'll study about dirigibles in preparation for our upcoming field trip to Sunnyvale."

Frightened for Connie, Hildy wasn't in the mood to think about the great airships. Still, she forced herself to concentrate on the teacher's instruction, because dirigibles were the essay topic for the scholarship competition.

"The great airships developed from free-floating hot-air balloons," the teacher began. "By 1901, in Paris, a one-man dirigible powered by a gasoline engine won a prize for covering a seven-mile distance in just over thirty minutes. However, Count von Zeppelin of Germany is credited with making the first really practical dirigible design."

Miss Krutz explained that Count Zeppelin had created rigid airships in place of the old hot-air balloons. By 1910, more than twenty years ago, Zeppelin's airships were carrying passengers. However, more than half of Zeppelin's dirigibles suffered disasters. Some burned. Others crashed in storms. And there have been some other tragedies, such as in landing operations.

"So you see," the teacher summarized, "dirigibles can be dangerous. How many of you have been to a talkie and seen a newsreel about a recent dirigible tragedy?"

Zelpha and her two friends raised their hands. Hildy guessed that the rest of the students, like herself, never had the nickel admission for a Saturday matinee.

Miss Krutz looked at Zelpha, Edna, and Tessie, then said, "You may remember seeing what happened as the *U.S.S. Akron* was coming in for a landing, and the wind caught it. Some line handlers holding on to the ship's cables—"

Zelpha interrupted without raising her hand. "I saw it! They were carried up into the air! Way high up! Some couldn't hang on until the dirigible was under control again, so they fell off and were killed."

Hildy shuddered, seeing in her mind's eye the terrible struggle of young men desperately trying to hang on to a long rope-like cable as the giant airship was swept up into the sky, out of control. Then Hildy visualized the sailors' strength giving out and their long fall to death far below the dirigible.

Her thoughts were interrupted by the door opening. She joined everyone else in turning to see a man stick his head into the room.

"Oh, Mr. Stanway!" the teacher greeted him. "Come in! Class, this is Mr. Emery Stanway, the man we've all been waiting to hear."

The Studebaker dealer was tall and slender with a smile that never faded. He moved so quickly he almost seemed to run across the front of the classroom. He swept off his tan Panama hat to make a tiny hint of a bow to the teacher.

"Miss Krutz," he said in a low, deep voice that seemed to make the desks vibrate, "how nice of you to again invite me to meet your illustrious class!"

Except for Mr. Farnham, Hildy had never seen another man who dressed as well. Yet the Studebaker dealer was flashy. Hildy recognized that the man's black and white leather shoes were similar to the ones she'd seen advertised for $2.29 in the "wish book," but Hildy was sure these shoes had cost at least $5.00.

Mr. Stanway's white shirt with pale blue pinstripes had the look of real silk. His navy blue suit with two-tone vest and pleated trousers surely cost more than the suits Hildy had seen advertised in the Sears catalog. Those ran from less than $10 up to almost $32. If there was a $40 suit, Hildy figured Mr. Stanway was wearing it.

He began his talk by pacing up and down in front of the class, the smile laced in place, the resonant voice filling the room.

"I see you're all looking at my attire. I couldn't always afford good clothes." He gently touched his fancy blue bow tie. "I had to quit school in the seventh grade. I worked in the fields, helping my folks make a living. I never went back to class."

He paused, his smile fading for the first time. "Instead, I worked for years, doing a man's job when I was still only a boy. I went down a long, long way before turning my life around. So today I'd like to tell you about what I learned the hard way, and then show you how what I'm saying now can be important all your life—if you'll listen and believe me."

Hildy leaned forward, feeling a kindred spirit with this man.

He continued. "One day when I was about fifteen and cleaning out a stable, a wise old farmer told me something that changed my life. He said, 'Emery, in good times or bad, some people get ahead, and some fall behind. It's each person's choice, and he or she can't blame anybody else. Just decide what it is you want, then figure out a way to do it, and never quit!"

Hildy shifted in her seat with rising excitement. *That's like Brother Ben said about Paul the Apostle! But what one thing do I want?*

Hildy didn't hear the rest of the man's story. Her thoughts leaped abruptly away from the schoolroom. *I want to win the scholarship. I want Connie found, for Ruby to stay here, and Spud to find a guardian so he can stay here too. I want Daddy to find a house so I can stay in this school. I want Zelpha to stop getting me in trouble.*

Hildy frowned, her mind still whirling. *But what one thing do I really want? One thing!*

That choice was easy.

After class, walking down the hallway with Ruby, Hildy was eager to tell Ruby about it. However, Hildy knew she first had to tell her cousin about the earlier conversation with Miss Krutz.

Ruby muttered, "If'n it'd a-been me, I'd a-told her that her dumb ol' niece writ the note! She probably stole it, too, figgerin' ye'd git blamed."

"I have faith it'll all work out." Hildy told Ruby about the thoughts she had during Mr. Stanway's talk. "Most of all, I want Connie found safe and sound. I also want that scholarship. But that's down the road, and Connie's in danger now. So I've got to help find her, while still trying to win the hundred dollars."

"How kin ye do that?"

"That's what I'll have to figure out. I have a feeling that part of the answer is down there on the river where that man and his dog chased us."

"Yore daddy done tol' ye to stay away from thar!"

"I know! But what would you do if you might be able to save Connie's life by going back down to the river?"

"Don't go tryin' to mix me up!"

The cousins stopped outside the classroom. Ruby studied Hildy hard, then observed, "Ye got that look in yore eyes! Yo're up to somethin', and it skeers me!"

Hildy took a slow, deep breath. "I've made a decision," she announced firmly.

Ruby groaned. "Don't tell me! I don't wanna know!"

Hildy nodded and started to enter the room.

Ruby stopped her. "Jist be careful, whatever it is."

"I'll be careful."

But will that be enough? Hildy wondered as she took her seat. Suddenly she was afraid.

CHAPTER THIRTEEN

WAITING FOR THE PHONE TO RING

Thursday

At noon, the cousins went downtown together so Hildy could buy school supplies with the money she'd made taking care of the Farnham children. The girls ate as they walked, the bright September sun reflecting off their shiny lunch buckets.

Hildy was thoughtfully silent, her eyes on the town clock three blocks to the east at Lone River's main intersection. The clock graced the top of the two-story, yellow-brick bank owned by Matthew Farnham. The large black Roman numerals stood out starkly against the white face, which was lighted, even in daytime. The old-fashioned hands seemed massive, yet Hildy could almost see them move.

Ruby asked, "Whatcha thinkin' about so hard?"

"The clock. It's strange how anything that seems so slow can move so fast."

"Yo're not makin' sense."

"Time, Ruby! Time! We've got exactly three days before the kidnapper's time limit runs out for Connie. But I've got to be in school instead of looking for her."

"I'm jist as sorry fer Connie as kin be, but neither of us kin do anythin' the menfolks cain't do." Ruby glanced around a little nervously. "I don't mean to rush ye none, but if'n that kidnapper's a-lookin' fer us, we ought to be off the streets as quick as we kin."

"I don't think we're in any real danger, especially with other kids and grown-ups around. But it won't do any harm to buy my supplies and get back to school. And I need some library books on dirigibles for my essay."

The visit to the dime store was completed quickly. Hildy took her newly purchased three-hole binder, straight pen, and compass back to the homeroom and put them in her desk.

The girls left their lunch pails in the cloakroom, then checked the small glass bookcase on the wall nearest the hallway. The school had no library, so each teacher had gathered what she could for her own class.

"There's not a single book here on dirigibles," Hildy complained. "Let's try the public library."

The girls hurried three blocks west to the library that was a gift of Andrew Carnegie. The late steel manufacturer had given money to build nearly three thousand libraries in towns like Lone River.

When Hildy had selected a couple of reference books on airships, she took them to the check-out desk. The plump librarian with flabby upper arms looked up. "I need your library card, please."

Hildy replied, "I don't have one."

"I see. Do either of your fathers own property?"

Hildy and Ruby shook their heads, not understanding what the question had to do with borrowing books.

"Sorry," the librarian said. "No property, no books."

Ruby snapped, "Ain't this a public lib'ary?"

"Yes," the librarian replied firmly, "But we've lost too many books to—uh—transients."

Hildy cried, "But that's unfair! I need those books to help in writing an essay for an important contest!"

"Rules are rules! If you want to sit over there at the table and read, you may. You can't check them out."

"I can't do that!" Hildy said in frustration. "I have to get back to school."

"We're open until six."

"I have to work after school."

"Sorry," the librarian said, and turned away.

Ruby's short temper started to erupt, but Hildy grabbed her cousin's arm and led her outside.

"Ye shoulda let me give her a good ol'-fashioned tongue-lashing!" Ruby fumed. "Actin' like we was dirt!"

"It's not her fault. She has to obey the rules," Hildy assured her cousin. "Someday they'll treat us differently. You'll see!"

"Ye mean, like that Studebaker feller?"

"Yes, and like Brother Ben and Mr. Farnham. They all started out poor. That's why the Farnhams let you and me work for them. They've been where we are, and they like to help others. So does Brother Ben and Mr. Stanway. Someday, when I get my education, I'll do the same. So can you, if you want."

"I don't have no fahr a-burnin' inside me," Ruby said with a shake of her blonde hair. "I like me jist like I am, and I ain't a-gonna change nothin', not even the way I talk. Shore, muh daddy's a-changin' on accounta he got religion an' turned to preachin'. But I ain't a-gonna. 'Sides, it tickles me to see how muh talk upsets some folks, like Miss Krutz and Mr. Wiley."

Hildy nodded, realizing that was true. She let her thoughts jump. Her eyes raised to the town clock.

"Time's running fast," she mused. "I wonder if the kidnapper's phoned the Farnhams."

"No way to know till ye git thar after school."

A few hours later when Hildy stepped off the old red bus in front of the Farnham mansion, Spud came to meet her.

"Any news?" Hildy asked as he unlocked the gate.

"Nothing. The Farnhams have been staying by the phone, but so far, no call from the kidnapper."

"Did they find anything last night at the river?"

"Not a thing. I stayed overnight. This morning Ben brought

in a friend who has some coon hounds, but they're not trained to find people. Since they left, I've been helping Mr. Farnham make some minor repairs around the barn. He comes out only for a few minutes, then goes back to stay with his wife and son, waiting for the phone to ring. Dickie's napping."

At the house Spud continued toward the barn while Hildy entered the big kitchen. She got a glimpse of Mr. Farnham in the hallway beyond.

Mrs. Farnham looked up from her wheelchair, where she was vigorously polishing silver. "Hi, Hildy," she said with a sad, weak voice. "I guess Spud told you Dickie's asleep?" When Hildy nodded, Mrs. Farnham added, "It's good for him. But Matt and I may never sleep again."

"Want me to do the polishing?"

"No, thanks. I'm doing it just to keep from going out of my mind, worrying about Connie, wondering why the kidnapper picked Sunday noon as a deadline, and trying to keep from screaming because he doesn't call!"

Hildy saw that the woman's eyes were red and swollen, with dark circles under them. Her face was drawn and crisscrossed with lines Hildy hadn't seen yesterday.

"I've been praying for Connie," Hildy said, still standing by the kitchen table. "For all of you."

"Thanks," Mrs. Farnham said with a voice that threatened to break. "So have we—Matt and I."

"What do you want me to do until Dickie wakes up?"

"I'm so distressed I don't know what to tell you. Do you have some homework or something you could do?"

"I have to research something about dirigibles, but I couldn't get any books or magazines to study."

"Look in the storage cabinet at the top of the stairs. Matt keeps all kinds of old magazines there."

The storage room smelled musty from being shut up so long. Hildy walked across the creaking uncarpeted floor between two walls filled with cardboard boxes neatly labeled.

Hildy opened the single window overlooking the back end of the property. She started to turn back to see if she could find any magazines or books on dirigibles.

Then she stopped, her eyes leaping from the bluff at the back end of the Farnham property, across the river, and onto the land beyond. The acres of corn stood in somber brown, their crops harvested. Dry stalks waited to be cut down.

Hildy lowered her gaze, trying to see the bluff where she and Ruby had been chased by the stranger and his dog. The cottonwoods and willows hid her objective.

She stood a moment, recalling details of how she and Ruby had wandered into the area by the bend of the river where the man and his dog had chased them.

Through the open window she could hear Spud hammering inside the barn. Hildy's gaze dropped to the woodpile. She saw in her mind's eye the tramp talking to Connie, heard in imagination her warning to the little girl about talking to strangers.

I wish I could get over this strange feeling about the stranger and his dog at the bend in the river! she thought. *Because I can't, I've got to go back down there and look. Daddy says I can't go alone, or with Ruby, but I've got to find a way! And fast! But how can I do it without disobeying Daddy?*

Hildy heard the grandfather clock downstairs musically chime the half hour. Hildy again stared thoughtfully toward the bend in the river with the cornfield beyond. Finally, she sighed, turned around, and began reading the box labels. They were mostly on banking and other financial subjects. One was marked *Magazines.*

She opened the box and sorted through the first half-dozen copies. The seventh had a dirigible photograph on the cover with the heading: DISASTROUS LEVIATHANS OF THE SKIES.

Hildy sat down on the floor, her back to the window for light, and against a stack of boxes. She started reading the article that focused on the sad history and tragedy of the monster airships.

The *U.S.S. Shenandoah* was the first dirigible filled with helium instead of highly explosive hydrogen. Caught in a 1925 lightning storm, the *Shenandoah* had broken in two.

In April, 1933, the *U.S.S. Akron* hit the surface of the sea and broke up.

Her sister ship, the *U.S.S. Macon*, christened only a short time before the *Akron* crashed, was still in service.

Hildy turned the page and blinked in surprise at a most startling photograph. It had been taken in 1927 of the dirigible *Los Angeles*. The huge ship was standing perfectly straight on its nose above Lakehurst's 160-foot mooring mast. The caption under the picture explained that the airship's tail had been caught by a sudden gust of wind. When the wind passed, the dirigible had settled down and been safely moored.

Hildy shook her head. *No wonder so many people think dirigibles aren't safe and want them stopped from flying!*

The phone downstairs rang. Hildy dropped her magazine and sat up. *Maybe it's the kidnapper!*

Hurrying down the stairs, senses alert, and heart speeding with anticipation, Hildy heard Mr. Farnham's voice through the closed parlor door.

"Yes," he said, "I'm writing it down."

Hildy didn't want to eavesdrop, but she was very anxious to know for sure if the kidnapper was on the other end of the line. Hildy opened the door to the kitchen and saw Mrs. Farnham in her wheelchair, listening to the extension.

"Is Connie all right?" the distraught mother asked anxiously. "Let me speak to . . . Yes, of course I want her back safely! Immediately!" She paused, then added dully, "All right, I'll hang up. But please, let me have my baby back safely!"

Hildy hurried across the room and looked down at the woman in the wheelchair. "What did he say?" Hildy asked.

Mrs. Farnham broke into sobs and lowered her face into her hands. Hildy knelt in front of her and tried to make out the muffled words, but couldn't.

Hildy looked up at the sound of the parlor door being opened quickly. She could hear Mr. Farnham's footsteps on the carpeted hallway as he ran out the side door and across the wooden porch. The screen door slammed behind him.

Dickie's muffled voice came from the distant bedroom. Hildy rose and rushed to where he sat sleepily in the bed.

"Is Connie home?" the boy asked anxiously.

"Not yet, but I think your father's going to get her. Come on, let's go see your mother."

Hildy led Dickie by the hand down the hallway toward the kitchen. She heard Mr. Farnham's Pierce Arrow accelerating past the house. Hildy opened the kitchen door just in time to look through the window and see Ben Strong's yellow Packard stopping outside.

She left Dickie with his mother and went to greet Ben at the back door. Spud, obviously alerted by the Pierce Arrow's sudden departure, arrived on the run from the barn. Hildy lowered her voice and briefly told what had just happened.

She and Spud followed Ben into the kitchen. The old man removed his hat, nodded politely to Mrs. Farnham, dropped the hat onto the rack by the door, and pulled a straightback chair from the table.

He sat down facing Mrs. Farnham and her son. Both were crying. The mother's upper body rocked back and forth in her wheelchair.

"Now, Beryl," Ben said in his soft drawl, "if you don't want to talk about it, we'll understand. But if you can tell us, we'd like to know what the kidnapper said."

Mrs. Farnham raised her bloodshot, teary eyes and looked past her son's head nestled against her breast. "He said to take the money in a paper bag and meet him at the culvert where the old River Road intersects with Franklin Road. He'd exchange Connie for the money. If Matt didn't come alone, or if anybody followed him, we'd never . . ." She broke off with a painful sob.

Hildy fought back tears that sprang, warm and unbidden, to her eyes. *That awful man! If he hurts Connie. . . !*

Ben fished a large silver pocket watch from his waistband and consulted it. "That's on a remote dirt road not very far from here. Matt should be back with Connie soon. Now, we wait and pray."

It was a long, painful wait. Hildy prayed silently while trying to get Dickie to leave his mother's lap. She was a frail woman whose thin, stricken leg did not support weight well. Hildy finally managed to get the boy to play quietly on the floor with some lead soldiers.

The others in the room sat or walked without speaking. Hildy watched the small clock over the high cupboard as the minutes ticked ominously by.

Fifteen minutes. Twenty. Twenty-five. Thirty.

He should have been back with Connie by now, Hildy thought, glancing at Spud and Ben.

They avoided her eyes. Still, Hildy knew they had also been watching the clock. She fought off a growing sense that something had gone wrong, but the terrible thought persisted.

Suddenly, Dickie stiffened and sat up on the linoleum. "Listen, it's Daddy!" He jumped up and dashed outside the back door.

Hildy ran after him. "Don't get in his way, Dickie!" She caught up with him and grabbed his hand as the Pierce Arrow passed through the gate, coming toward the house.

Hildy strained to see through the windshield. She stared hard, seeing the bag of money was on the front seat, but there was no sign of Connie. Hildy groaned, realizing Mr. Farnham had returned with the ransom because the kidnapper hadn't met him with the little girl.

Through the open kitchen window, Hildy heard Mrs. Farnham let out a soul-wrenching scream.

Hildy gasped, "He's alone! Connie's not with him!"

Chapter Fourteen

PUTTING FEET TO FAITH

Thursday Night and Friday Morning

It was late when Ben drove Hildy home. She was shocked and silent after learning that Connie was still a kidnap victim. Worst of all, according to the kidnapper's note, time was running out for Connie.

Doubts began attacking Hildy. *Why didn't God ever answer our prayers? Maybe it does no good to pray.*

The old Ranger seemed to read her thoughts. In the darkness of the Packard's interior, he said, "Faith's a strange thing, Hildy. But we mustn't lose it, because it's the key to a good life, both now and hereafter."

Hildy nodded but didn't answer.

"Of course," Ben explained in his soft drawl, "we have to put feet to faith when we can. I've been doing that. For instance, I've quietly checked at the big Piggly Wiggly's store downtown, and the four little corner groceries around Lone River. Guess what I learned?"

Hildy's curiosity stirred. "What?"

"None of the butchers remembered anybody coming in just

to get some paper. That doesn't surprise me. The kidnapper probably found an old discarded piece on which to paste his note."

"You know that little shack that Stan and Elsie Marden built as a corner store at the east edge of town?"

It was walking distance from the mansion. "Yes. Why?"

"Well, somebody's broken in there twice in the last two weeks. Didn't take any money, just some food. Things that wouldn't spoil—crackers, tinned meat, and so forth."

Hildy sat up, suddenly very interested. "You think maybe the kidnapper. . . ?"

"If it had happened only once, I'd say maybe some poor man down on his luck did it. But he'd probably have taken the money left in the cigar box they keep under the counter for a cash register. He'd have taken bread and maybe baloney to eat right away.

"There's something else I've done that put action to my faith. You know how the telephone system in this town works?"

Hildy shook her head, so the old Ranger explained. "Nellie Grimes has the switchboard in her home. Every call that's made in Lone River goes through that board. She has two cords with plugs on them. There are so few telephones around that she knows where each call originates.

"In other words, when a call comes in, she can tell what phone it's coming from. So she plugs in the first cord and says, 'Operator.' The person calling tells her which subscriber number is wanted. Or sometimes the caller just gives the name of the person, without a number. Anyway, Nellie plugs in the second cord to that subscriber's number, completing the circuit."

"Oh," Hildy said, "now I understand something that happened the first day at school. When the principal asked his secretary to make a call from his office, I heard her say, 'Nellie, would you get me the Farnham residence?' So, Brother Ben, you're saying this Nellie could look at her switchboard and know it was the school calling, even if Miss Perkins didn't say who it was?"

"Yup! In that case, after Nellie plugged both cords into two little round holes on her board—that's called patching—Mr. Wiley was connected to Matt and Beryl's number. Nellie then flipped a little switch with her finger, and the phone rang at the Farnhams'."

Hildy's mind raced. "That means when the kidnapper called their house this afternoon, Nellie could have known where it originated? Even which phone he used?"

"Yup! Even a pay phone. So Nellie and I had agreed— nobody else knows—that she would mark down the origin and time of every call to Matt's home."

Hildy cried joyfully, "Oh, Brother Ben!"

"Since the kidnapper didn't show up to meet Matt, I'm hoping he'll call again. If he does, and he uses the same phone— even if it's a pay one, which I suspect—I'll know where he called from. If he doesn't have a car, he's probably walking to the nearest phone."

When Hildy entered the barn-house, she was feeling much better. She came in quietly, expecting everyone to be asleep. She wasn't surprised to see that the kerosene light had been turned down low for her, but she hadn't expected to see her father and stepmother waiting up.

Hildy slid wearily onto the bench facing them and briefly reported the discouraging developments at the Farnham mansion. However, at Ben's request, she had agreed not to tell anyone about the stolen food or Nellie Grimes.

Hildy concluded, "Mr. Farnham said he followed the directions exactly, so he doesn't know why the kidnapper didn't show up. They're just hoping he'll call again."

Molly whispered, "Oh, those poor people!"

Hildy's father turned the flame up higher on the lamp. "Since that's happened, Hildy, maybe we'd better talk some more about you wanting to go back down the river where you kids were chased. You still want to do that?"

"Yes! I can't explain it, but I have this funny feeling that there's a tie-in with what Ruby and I saw and Connie's disappearance."

"You said adults had searched the river again today—even

with dogs—and found nothing that even hinted you're right. Now I know you can be bullheaded . . ."

"Joe!" Molly reproved him, laying a hand on his arm.

"It's okay," Hildy said, looking at her stepmother with a faint smile. "I guess I've always had a mind of my own. Daddy and I've had this discussion before. It doesn't hurt my feelings. I know he doesn't mean it in a bad way."

Joe smiled at his daughter. "Your mother used to say you had the courage of your convictions. She and I sometimes went around and around on whether she was right or I was. Anyway, I started to say that if you're really convinced that there's something down at the river that could help find that little girl, I guess I'd better let you look—but I'll go with you."

"You will? When?"

"Tomorrow, maybe. Anyway, the sooner the better. Since the kidnapper didn't keep his word today, Connie's life is probably in even more danger than it was. You and Ruby may be in danger, too."

"I don't really think we are, Daddy."

"Just the same, we'll all feel better when this is over. Since Matt Farnham's such an important man around here, the Woods Brothers volunteered to let some of us riders go help search for Connie. They don't know she's been kidnapped. They just think she's lost. Anyway, I'm one of those riders."

"Oh, Daddy! I'm so glad!"

"I'll ask to search along the river bottom in back of Farnham's. Naturally, I'll have to look like a hunter in case the kidnapper sees us. So I'll carry a shotgun and walk. Riding would look suspicious. Oh, maybe you'd better borrow some of Ruby's overalls and a hat so you'll look like a boy in case the man sees you."

"Then he'd think we were a father and son hunting quail or something. Oh, Daddy, thank you!"

"I'll try to be there tomorrow afternoon after school. There's no way I can let you know ahead of time, so I'll show up at the Farnhams if I can. If something happens at the ranch and I can't get away, we'll try again Saturday. Ask Ruby to take care of Dickie for you."

Hildy asked about the possible house to rent near the one-room school. Her father said there was nothing new to report. Then he stood up and suggested they all get some sleep.

Everyone was in their bedding and the lamp blown out when Hildy's father spoke softly in the darkness. "Hildy, you know I'm not a man to say a whole lot of pretty words."

"I know."

There was a silence, and Hildy suspected her father had chosen the darkness to say things that would have been impossible for him in a face-to-face situation.

"I've never said it before, Hildy," the voice came huskily across the darkened barn-house, "but I'm proud of you."

Hildy felt a sudden warmth in the back of her eyes. She wanted to answer, but didn't know what to say. She swallowed hard and waited.

"What I mean," her father continued, "is I know how much you want—not to live like this."

Hildy suspected his eyes were sweeping the poverty of the darkened barn-house interior, his ears taking in sounds of five children lightly snoring on their pallets.

"I do the best I can," he said, his voice barely audible, "but living like this doesn't bother me as it does you. You're different. I've known that since you were a little girl. You've got something that makes you see things I can't see, sort of like dreams that make you believe that you can have what you see in your head."

Joe was again silent for a moment while Hildy waited. "What I'm trying to say," her father spoke again, his voice stronger, more sure, "is that I know it doesn't matter where a person was born—like Jesus in a manger and you in a sharecropper's cabin.

"What counts is what you believe. You believe you've got a special purpose in life. I never had that. But you do, and I know that you're not going to stay in the same condition in which you were born. So it doesn't matter where you were born. It's where you end up that counts. I know you're going to climb high. I'm proud to be your father."

When the silence had stretched out long enough so Hildy knew her father wasn't going to say anything more, she whispered, "Thank you, Daddy."

He didn't reply. Hildy lay awake a long time, savoring words never heard before. Slowly, these gave way to concern for Connie and the other problems facing Hildy. Finally, she folded her hands on her chest and looked up at the rafters invisible in the night. Her lips moved, but the prayer was silent, deep in her heart.

———

The next morning in homeroom, Hildy guessed that by noon Ben Strong would have learned from Nellie Grimes what phone the kidnapper had used yesterday. Maybe Ben would come by and tell Hildy during the lunch hour. She was also eager for the school day to be over so she could go with her father to the river. Most of all, Hildy thought about Connie and why the kidnapper had failed to keep his appointment with Mr. Farnham.

Hildy was forced to break off her thoughts when Miss Krutz exhibited pictures of Germany's *Graf Zeppelin* and said students might wish to take notes for their essays as she explained more about the giant airship.

Hildy picked up the unfamiliar straight pen, removed the cork from her inkwell and dipped the point into the black ink. She got too much on the point. A big drop plopped onto her lined note paper and spattered messily.

She heard a snicker and looked up to see both Tessie and Edna smirking at her. Hildy used her blotter, but one big ugly stain and many little ones remained on her paper. However, she had no time to worry about such things, because Miss Krutz's lesson was being given fast.

Hildy wrote furiously, hearing the scratching of the pen and occasionally seeing tiny droplets fly off the point to splatter on the paper. If neatness counted, Hildy would have preferred the familiar lead pencil. But she was growing up, and a seventh grader needed to know how to master a persnickety straight pen.

When the period was nearly over, the teacher suggested that the students look over the notes they'd taken.

Hildy was distressed at her messy paper, but realized she

had slowly improved her skill with the pen by the time she had finished. Her eyes skimmed her notes.

- Graf Zeppelin launched 6 years ago. Crossed Atlantic with passengers.
- Last year, docked at Akron, Ohio.
- Cruised at 73 miles an hour. Seated 16 people for dinner. Two rows of sleeping cabins; 10 total.
- Left Germany with 23 passengers, 40 crewmen.
- Crossed Atlantic in 5 days. Survived 2 storms.
- Arrived U.S. Naval Air Station Lakehurst, N.J.
- Covered 6,200 miles in just under 112 hours.
- Between 300 and 500 men needed to land Graf.
- A year later, Graf circled world in 12 days. 20,500 miles.

Hildy laid her pen down in the slot at the top of her desk and flexed her stiff fingers. She looked again at her notes and frowned.

Dull words! she told herself. *It needs something exciting if I'm going to write a composition good enough to win the scholarship.* Then she shrugged. *Oh, well, I've got time to think of something different. But there's not much time left to find Connie. That's the most important thing right now. Maybe Daddy and I can help find her this afternoon.*

In the hallway after first period, Hildy and Ruby started for their next class, but Zelpha stopped them. Tessie and Edna stood behind her.

"Why'd you take all those notes?" Zelpha demanded of Hildy. "Ruby hardly took any at all."

Ruby snapped, "Not that it's any of yore beeswax, but I'm not interested in writin' no essay. But she is, and she's a-gonna win that thar hunnert dollars!"

Zelpha ignored Ruby and continued to look at Hildy, her eyes filled with emotion. "You haven't got a prayer of writing a decent essay! Why, you can't even write properly with a pen."

"I'm getting better," Hildy replied. She thought about adding that the scholarship was not her immediate concern. But Hildy didn't dare do that because Zelpha would probably want to know why, and Hildy couldn't talk about Connie being kidnapped.

"Getting better?" Zelpha rolled her eyes as if to say that was unbelievable. "I've seen your kind before. They come like tumbleweeds, roll in, stop awhile, then blow on. I didn't like them, and I don't like you!"

Hildy felt Ruby tense, so Hildy reached out quickly and gripped her cousin's arm in silent warning. "I'm sorry you don't," Hildy said evenly. "I just wish I could figure out why you dislike me."

"You don't know?" Zelpha demanded, her voice rising. She turned to Tessie and Edna. "She doesn't know why!"

Hildy heard Ruby take a quick, sharp breath and knew her cousin was about to lose her short temper. Hildy again spoke quickly. "I guess it's because you think you're better than we are."

"You guess?" Zelpha cried so loud that other students walking by turned to look. "You live in a *barn!*"

Hildy felt her mouth go dry. "That's only temporary," she said, fighting to keep her voice calm, "just like the sharecropper's cabin where I was born was only temporary! My daddy says it doesn't matter where you were born as long as you know where you're going."

"My daddy says!" Zelpha interrupted in a high, mocking tone. "My daddy says!" She returned to her own voice, but with anger tingeing it. "Well, I don't care what yours says! It's my father I have to think about!" Zelpha turned suddenly and almost ran down the hallway. Her two friends trailed her.

Ruby asked, "What in the world got her so het up?"

Hildy stared thoughtfully after Zelpha. "I don't know, but I wish I did."

Zelpha's outburst disturbed Hildy, but she was more concerned about joining her father that afternoon to search for Connie. Time was going by fast, because only two days remained before the kidnapper's deadline.

CHAPTER FIFTEEN

THE STRANGER RETURNS

Friday

The cousins started walking fast toward their next class. Ruby said, "I talked some about Zelpha to muh daddy. He thinks maybe yo're some kinda threat to her. Like maybe yo're a-standin' in her way."

Hildy considered that, then shook her head. "I think it has something to do with Zelpha's father. I've got to learn more about him."

Hildy's first chance to do that came that afternoon when she and Ruby arrived at the Farnhams'. Ruby usually did housework on Saturday, but because she wanted to go to Thunder Mountain with her father that day, she'd obtained Mrs. Farnham's permission to come after school on Friday. That also tied in with Hildy's plans to have Ruby watch Dickie if Hildy's father arrived to help search for Connie.

Hildy and Ruby entered the mansion to see Mr. and Mrs. Farnham sitting by the kitchen telephone, nervously waiting for the kidnapper to call again. Both parents looked haggard and tired. They obviously hadn't slept much last night.

Mrs. Farnham gave Ruby instructions on her work and asked Hildy to take Dickie outside.

Hildy led the boy to the barn, where Spud was pitching alfalfa into Robin's stall. When Dickie started playing on stacked bales of hay, Hildy walked close to the manger so she could watch the little boy while talking to Spud.

She lowered her voice so Dickie couldn't hear. "It's hard just to stand here instead of trying to find Connie. But my daddy's going to try coming over later. We'll go to the river where I've been wanting to look."

Spud plunged the pitchfork into a full bale of hay and bent to cut the wires with a pair of pliers. "I went looking down there today with the deputy dressed in plain clothes," he said. "He brought along a coon hunter with a bloodhound that was supposed to be able to trail lost people. The dog couldn't pick up Connie's scent. If she is down there, the trail is cold.

"The deputy also said if the man who chased you and Ruby was still there, that big brindle dog would have barked at them or at the bloodhound. The deputy thinks the man is long gone from there, and so's his dog."

Hildy felt a terrible sadness and frustration that left her unwilling to talk more about the missing girl.

Hildy walked to the door and looked toward the driveway. She hoped Ben would drive up and report on what Nellie Grimes had learned of the phone the kidnapper had used yesterday. Hildy also wanted to tell Spud what Ben's detective work had turned up, but she had promised to keep it quiet, even from Ruby and Spud.

Remembering Zelpha's remarks about her father, Hildy walked back over to Spud, who was breaking loose the alfalfa bale. She asked, "Did Brother Ben or Mr. Farnham ever talk to you about a man named Karl Krutz?"

Spud took off his aviator cap and wiped his brow with the back of a large, freckled hand. "No, nobody's said anything, but I've heard things."

"Such as?"

"Well, Karl Krutz owns the Lone River Bakery. He's also president of the school board of trustees. Runs things with an iron hand. Scares everybody who works for him at the bakery or the school. Why do you ask?"

Hildy told about Zelpha's outburst that morning, then added, "I'm sure there's something more important than the scholarship involved. Zelpha doesn't need the hundred dollars that much, because her father's fairly well off. So she must have another motive."

"What's that got to do with her father?"

"I don't know. Just a hunch."

Spud replaced his aviator cap and again picked up the pitchfork. "Don't ask me to understand fathers."

"I've been thinking. Maybe in some way Zelpha needs that scholarship more than I, and I'm standing in her way. Am I being selfish? No matter how much I want that scholarship, maybe Zelpha needs it more—for reasons I don't understand. I'd like to tell her that as much as I need that money, it's not as important to me as having Connie returned safely.

"I sure hope Daddy gets here this afternoon! The kidnapper's deadline is now less than forty-four hours away."

Hildy walked to the barn window and looked out toward the distant bend in the river. "Maybe Daddy and I'll find something," she said hopefully.

Spud leaned the pitchfork in a corner and sat down on a bale of hay. "I've been giving this whole matter a lot of thought," he began. "Do you think an ordinary tramp knows enough to plan a kidnapping?"

Hildy walked over and sat down by him, facing Dickie, who was still playing by himself. "What do you think?"

Spud shrugged. "Maybe he wasn't just a hobo. There are millions of men out of work in this country. Some were ordinary day laborers, but others were college professors and accountants. Like any group of men, some are not as honest as others. Some may be desperate enough to risk a kidnapping.

"So maybe the one who took Connie saw this mansion first, and decided to burglarize it. But when he came to the door looking for a handout and saw only a woman in a wheelchair and two little kids here by themselves most of the day, he figured it'd be easy to get a lot more money by holding one of the children for ransom."

"Mrs. Farnham did tell me she'd seen that tramp here a couple of weeks before he came back the day I saw him," Hildy said.

"Maybe he had another motive," Spud said. "Maybe he got mad when Mrs. Farnham ran him off, and he decided on revenge. What worse thing could he do than take one of her children?"

Hildy looked sharply at Spud, and he added hastily, "Okay, so it'd be worse if—if they didn't ever get her back."

Hildy shuddered. "She's got to be found—and fast! I hope Daddy gets here before it's too dark to look!"

"Suppose he doesn't?"

Hildy considered that. "Well, he did take back what he said about my not going down there. He just wanted to go with me." She glanced at Spud. "So I think it'd be all right if you, Ruby, and I went together."

Spud slowly shook his head. "I don't know."

"We're racing against the clock, Spud! We really have no choice! If the Farnhams don't hear from the kidnapper, and my father's not here when it's time for Ruby and me to quit work, then we can all go to the river. That way, we'll all be safe." She added under her breath, "I hope."

The kidnapper had not called by the time Hildy and Ruby were to leave work for the day. Hildy returned Dickie to the care of his parents while silently fretting about why Brother Ben hadn't shown up.

Hildy said to Ruby, "Wonder what's keeping Daddy? If he doesn't get here pretty soon, it'll be too dark to go searching." Hildy hesitated a moment, then suggested that Ruby join her and Spud in going back down to the river to look for Connie.

"Nuh-uh!" Ruby said emphatically, shaking her head so hard the short blonde hair bounced. "I told ye I ain't never goin' back! I don't want no ol' dawg a-chompin' on my leg bones, 'specially when it's gittin' towards dark."

"Well, Spud and I are still going!" Hildy replied. "We're not going to leave any stone unturned in trying to find Connie before it's too late."

Ruby scowled at Hildy, but her tone was mild. "If'n yo're a-tryin' to make me feel guilty as sin, ye shore air a-doin' a good job of it! Oh, all right! If'n Uncle Joe ain't here in fifteen minutes, I'll go with y'all."

Twenty minutes later, with Lindy bounding ahead, Hildy, Ruby, and Spud headed across the bottom land toward the river. The late September sun was already starting to slip well down the western sky, making the big valley oaks cast long shadows ahead of the trio.

"We'll have to hurry," Hildy said, casting an anxious glance at the sky. "We'd better go directly to the bend in the river."

"Yo're bound and determined to go whar that mean ol' dawg's a-waitin' to eat us alive," Ruby protested.

"Ah," Spud scoffed, "he can't be too bad. Why, when I tramped across the country, sleeping in hobo jungles or going up to some farmhouse to ask for a handout, I saw dogs so big they looked almost like ponies."

"I ain't interested in yore life story!" Ruby snapped, ducking under a low-hanging oak limb.

"Cut it out, you two!" Hildy said sternly. "We're getting close enough that we'd better be quiet."

Spud lowered his voice. "Lindy'll let us know if anybody's around."

A few minutes later, the Airedale stopped and sniffed. Hildy, Spud, and Ruby also stopped.

Hildy felt a little ripple of fear start on the back of her neck. She watched anxiously as Lindy quartered forward, following his nose to a patch of wild blackberry vines about eight feet high, twenty feet across, and fifty yards long.

Hildy's mind whirled. *I never thought of that! A person could cut a small hole down low in those vines, then crawl deep inside. Nobody'd see . . .*

Lindy barked sharply and again stopped, his nose toward the vines.

Cautiously, Hildy, Ruby, and Spud eased forward.

Ruby wrinkled her nose. "Whew! Something's daid!"

Hildy turned away. "Sure is!"

Spud whispered, "You two stay here." He eased forward while Hildy and Ruby stood still under the shelter of a three-hundred-year-old valley oak.

Spud stopped behind his dog and stretched his neck to peer ahead of him. Then he called softly to Lindy and returned to the girls.

"What. . . ?" Hildy began, then stopped, unable to finish the question for fear of the possible answer.

"You don't have to worry anymore about that big tiger-striped dog," Spud said.

The girls exchanged startled glances. Then Hildy frowned. "What happened to him?"

"It's hard to say. Anyway, now we know why the searchers haven't seen or heard the dog that chased you girls. And we don't have to worry about him."

"Jist that stranger!" Ruby mumbled under her breath. "With his big ol' spear!"

Hildy urged, "Don't worry about that! Just try to think about finding and saving Connie."

Spud suggested, "If we do get pursued, let's split up. We'll be safer that way."

Hildy nodded but didn't say anything. She had an uneasy feeling that even if they were chased, and all three went in different directions, the stranger would keep after her. She just hoped she could outrun him.

The trio went on toward the bend in the river with the cornfield above the chalky bluff. But now they walked in silence, sobered by the discovery of the big dog, yet relieved he was no longer a menace. The fast-disappearing daylight was a growing concern.

Hildy broke the silence with a low comment. "We'd better stay behind these oaks as much as possible until we get to the cottonwoods. Then maybe we should stop and look around really well before going to the river."

The others nodded, automatically bending over and moving on tiptoes. They paused at the first cottonwood with its rough, scaly bark. Everyone crouched down in silence, eyes searching for any movement.

Overhead, Hildy heard the yellowing leaves rustling and making a scary sound in the light breeze. The fragrance of the nearby willows mixed with the distinctive smell of the shallow, rushing river.

For at least a minute, nobody spoke. Hildy watched Lindy as he tested the air with his black nose, showing no other signs of alertness; he was just a dog enjoying being with his master and friends.

"Guess it's safe," Hildy said. "Let's go on to the willows by the river. Then we can spread out but keep in sight of each other. Look for signs of where there's been a campfire, food, or tin cans that aren't yet rusted."

Spud added, "Watch for some kind of shelter where the tramp could be holding Connie—a wooden shack, the body of an old car or wagon bed, a cardboard shelter, even one made of gunnysacks. Look for tracks . . ."

He broke off as Lindy suddenly tensed, swiveled his head upstream and started to growl.

"Quiet, Lindy!" Spud whispered urgently. He reached out and clamped a big freckled hand over the dog's muzzle so he could breathe but not bark. "Somebody's coming!"

"Everybody down!" Hildy urged in a hoarse whisper.

The three friends dropped out of sight, eyes straining to see what the dog already knew was coming.

Hildy realized that the sun was down and the river area was filling with dark shadows. Her heart sped up as she remembered being chased by the stranger and his dog. Then Hildy relaxed, aware the dog was no longer a threat.

Her complacency was immediately destroyed, because Spud whispered, "Must be close! Look at Lindy!"

Hildy glanced down at the Airedale. He started to bristle, hair standing on end along his neck and shoulders. Hildy heard a low rumble in his chest.

Hildy shifted her gaze back to the river. Peering beyond the willows at the river's edge, she glimpsed a movement in the shallows just off the nearby shore. She strained to see better.

Slowly, she made out a man wading in the river. He carried a three-pointed spear. He suddenly stopped and looked toward the hidden trio.

Ruby gasped, "That's him! The same man! An' he's a-comin' this way!"

CHAPTER SIXTEEN

WAITING BEGINS AGAIN

Friday Night and Saturday Morning

Hildy reached out to give her cousin a warning squeeze on her arm, but it was too late.

Ruby whispered, "He's a-comin' straight fer us with that spear!"

"Shh!" Spud hissed.

Ruby snapped, "Don't tell me what to do!"

"Quiet! Both of you!" Hildy said firmly.

They obeyed, crouching beside Hildy, watching the unshaven, dirty-looking tramp wading through the shallow water toward their hiding place.

Hildy tensed, ready to signal for Ruby and Spud to turn and run. The man stopped, lifted the spear, and plunged it into the water. Hildy glimpsed a V-shaped ripple on the surface as a large salmon darted away with a flash of silvery sides.

"He missed a salmon," Hildy whispered as the man turned away from the shore. "He's going on."

The stranger continued his slow, steady way through the shallows across the stream. Hildy relaxed. "He's too far away, and he can't hear us above the sound of the river," she said.

The stranger gave no sign of hearing or seeing the hidden trio. In the fast-falling twilight, he waded past the bluff, around the bend, and out of sight downstream.

Hildy straightened up. "Come on! Let's see where he's going."

Spud released Lindy's nose with a warning to be quiet. Then he and Ruby followed Hildy in a tiptoed, bent-over advance past the white bluff and around the river's bend.

There Hildy stopped, her eyes glancing everywhere. "Hey, where'd he go?"

Spud took off his aviator cap and scratched his head. "He just disappeared into thin air!"

Ruby leaned closer to Hildy and whispered, "Maybe it wasn't a man a-tall, but a haint!"

"Ruby!" Hildy said reprovingly. "How many times have I told you there's no such thing as a haunt?"

"Jist the same, I'm a-gittin' outta here!" Ruby turned away from the river.

Hildy glanced nervously at the deepening shadows of dusk. "Maybe we had better go back," she said and followed Ruby. Spud and Lindy trailed behind.

When they were safely inside the Farnhams' property, they stopped on top of the bluff to catch their breath.

Ruby panted, "Ye kin say what ye want, but I still think it was a haint!"

Spud growled disapprovingly, "I can't see how any right-thinking person could be so superstitious!"

"Ye a-sayin' I cain't think straight?" Ruby asked.

Hildy pleaded, "Please stop that! You're forgetting the important thing—the kidnapper is still down there!"

Spud shook his head. "You're assuming that the man we saw and the kidnapper are the same person, but you don't have any proof of that. Maybe the man we saw was just what he seemed to be, a hobo spearing salmon."

Hildy looked at Spud, now only a dark silhouette against the western horizon. "He didn't have any fish, and the spear could be a weapon."

Ruby asked, "Then why'd he wade in the river?"

Hildy replied, "I think he was walking there so he wouldn't leave any tracks. And he moved like a man who knew where he was going."

"Where *was* he going?" Spud inquired.

"Obviously, to some place that we couldn't see. Maybe that's why the other searchers haven't found him."

Spud agreed. "It's certain that he just didn't disappear. He had to come out of the water someplace right around the bend in the river. But that doesn't prove he had anything to do with Connie's disappearance."

"There's one way to make sure," Hildy said, looking again toward the river, now totally engulfed in darkness. We've got to go back down there again and wait until he goes around the bend, so we can see how he vanishes."

Ruby sputtered, "Ye plumb crazy? That spear he was a-carryin' ain't no toy!"

Hildy replied gently, "You're forgetting that there's a little four-year-old girl out there somewhere, and I'm sure that man knows where she is! Don't you see? We've got to go back and do what I said! Connie's life may depend on it!"

Ruby sighed. "Like I said before, if'n yo're a-tryin' to make me feel guilty as sin, ye shore air a-doin' a good job of it. Guess I kin risk goin' ag'in."

As the trio neared the mansion, now only a black hulk against the night, Hildy wondered why her father had not shown up. She also wondered if Brother Ben had come and gone. She was anxious to know what he'd learned from Nellie Grimes. But Hildy was even more anxious to learn if Connie's kidnapper had called the Farnhams. She wanted to tell them that the tramp and suspected kidnapper had just been seen again, only to vanish almost before their eyes.

Hildy led Ruby and Spud in sprinting across the Farnhams' spacious backyard lawn toward the mansion. Hildy reached the kitchen ahead of Ruby and Spud. The Farnhams were just entering that room from the interior hallway. The banker held on to his son with his left hand and pushed his wife's wheelchair with the other. Hildy saw at once that something had happened.

Dickie blurted, "Connie's coming home!"

His father gently corrected him. "Her abductor just called again. He said that the first time he was just testing to see if I'd follow orders, bring the money, and come alone. Just now he said he'd phone again first thing in the morning with the exact time and place to exchange the ransom for Connie."

Mrs. Farnham exclaimed, "Oh, I hope he keeps his word! I couldn't stand another failure! I just couldn't!"

Her husband reached over the back of her wheelchair and gave her a pat on the shoulder. "It'll be all right. I'm sure he'll come through this time. It's logical he'd want to get the ransom money and leave this area as fast as possible." Mr. Farnham looked at Hildy and Ruby. "Since tomorrow is Saturday, could you girls be here early to help out?"

"I can," Hildy replied, "but Ruby planned to go up to Thunder Mountain with her father."

"Jist now changed muh mind," Ruby said. "I cain't go off till Connie's found."

Hildy was relieved. She smiled at her cousin, then turned to the banker. "Did he say Connie's all right?"

Mr. Farnham nodded. "Yes, but he wouldn't let us talk to her. Now, girls, I'm sorry we can't say anything more, because he warned us not to. If you two are ready, I'll drive you home. Spud, I'd appreciate it if you and Lindy would keep an eye on my wife and son."

On the drive, Hildy told Mr. Farnham about the experience she, Ruby, and Spud had shared on the river.

The banker said grimly, "Beryl and I are grateful for what you three have done. If we hadn't heard from the kidnapper just now, I'd be inclined to take lights and turn that river bottom upside down until we found where he disappeared. But since we were promised that Connie would be safely returned tomorrow, I'm afraid of doing anything that might upset those plans."

Hildy understood. She let her mind jump to the telephone operator and Brother Ben. *Now he'll have two phone calls that Nellie Grimes will know about. I wonder where they were made? Oh, I wish Brother Ben would show up so I could at least know about the first one!*

Hildy's thoughts jumped again, while strong emotions seized her. *That poor little girl! Spending another night with the man who kidnapped her! She's sure to be scared to death! She might even be hurt. And she's too young to understand why she can't be home with her family. Yet we're all so helpless! And the deadline's almost here! If anything goes wrong with that meeting tomorrow . . .*

Ruby interrupted Hildy's thoughts. "Mr. Farnham, after ye git Connie back, ye reckon her kidnapper will be caught a-fore he gits plumb away?"

Mr. Farnham answered, "I don't dare call in the federal agents, because of the kidnapper's threat, but as soon as we have my daughter back, I'll notify the FBI. They'll get him!"

As Hildy entered the barn-house, her father looked up. His right arm was in a sling.

"Daddy! What happened?" Hildy ran to him and bent to see by lamplight.

"Horse fell on me. Arm's not broken, but the foreman took me into town so ol' Doc Carson could look at it. Sorry I couldn't get out to help you look for that man."

Like most people in hard times, Joe Corrigan would not have gone to a doctor on his own because of the cost. Insurance was unheard of. The Woods Brothers were unusual in that they took good care of their employees.

When Hildy was satisfied that her father was all right, she sat down on the bench and told him and Molly what had happened that afternoon at the Farnhams'.

When Hildy had finished, her father commented, "I hope they get their little girl back safely in the morning. But there's nothing we can do now except wait."

"And pray," his wife added quietly.

Joe didn't seem to hear, but Hildy knew he had. He seldom said anything about spiritual matters.

"Hildy," he said with a stern tone that made her wince, "I

told you I'd take you down to the river as soon as I could, and I meant it. But . . ."

Hildy interrupted, "I didn't go alone! I told you that Ruby and Spud were with me!"

Her father's voice took on a sharp edge. "You risked your life, and Ruby's and Spud's, by going down there!"

"But, Daddy, you only said Ruby and I couldn't go alone! Spud and Lindy went too! Besides, Connie's . . ."

"Don't interrupt! You know better than that!"

Molly cautioned, "Shh, Joe! You'll wake the kids!"

Hildy lowered her eyes and waited a moment. When her father was silent, she spoke again. "Daddy, I didn't mean to disobey! I had such a strong feeling—although I can't explain it—that we could find and save Connie. I didn't think there'd be any real danger with Ruby and Spud along."

Her father reached out and gently laid a rough, work-calloused hand against her bare forearm. "Well, I guess it doesn't matter, because tomorrow the Farnhams will have their girl back."

"I hope you're right, although the last time . . ." She broke off her sentence and finished, "But tomorrow I pray that everything turns out right and this whole nightmare will be over."

Molly whispered, "Amen," then raised her voice. "Joe, tell her about the house."

Hildy turned expectantly to her father. Her heart started to sink with dread.

"Oh, yeah. While I was waiting at the doc's, one of the others waiting was the landlord of that place near the one-room school. He's decided not to rent to anybody with a bunch of kids."

Hildy almost shouted with relief, although she felt sorry for her father.

He continued, "While the doc was fixing my arm, I was carrying on about having to move by the first and having no place to go. Doc told me about a place right down the road apiece. I went by and looked at it, then came here and took your mother to see it."

He paused, leaving Hildy up in the air.

Molly added, "It's not much, but it's better than this barn-house. It's partly furnished too. Got some real bedsprings, an old kitchen stove, some beat-up chairs, and a couple chests of drawers. But fifteen dollars a month is a lot of money."

Hildy couldn't stand it anymore. She cried, "Did you get it?"

Molly nodded. "I liked it, so your father made a deal with the landlord to let us move in, then give him the first month's rent after Joe gets paid."

Hildy exclaimed, "You mean I can still go to the same school?"

"Sure can!" her father assured her. "You can keep Mischief too."

That night Hildy crawled into her pallet with her faith beginning to grow. She prayed silently, expressing her gratitude, but added a prayer for the problems that still lay ahead.

Hildy awoke with the eager anticipation that soon Connie would be safely home. Yet as she dressed and started walking toward the Farnhams', an uneasy feeling gripped her.

She had reached the Lombardy poplars at the end of the lane, when Ruby arrived with her father in the Model T. "My, Uncle Nate," Hildy exclaimed, "you look swell!"

He was freshly shaven and his hair was slicked down with an oil that gave off a rose fragrance. He looked very nice in his brown suit, white shirt, and flowered green tie. Hildy could smell the stove-blacking he'd used to polish his shoes.

"Thanks," he replied, smiling. "Get in. I'll drop both you gals off at the Farnhams'."

Ruby shot Hildy a meaningful glance. "He's a-gonna see the Widder Benton."

Hildy nodded, already knowing that. "Give her my regards," she said. "And the kids." She paused, then asked, "When are you going to make a decision about whether to accept that call to the Ozark church?"

"Ask me when I get back tonight," he said.

At the Farnhams', Hildy and Ruby started to enter the back screen door just as Dickie rushed out of the kitchen toward them. His eyes were wide with excitement. "Daddy's talking to that man on the phone!"

The cousins didn't have to ask whom the boy meant. Hildy grabbed his hand and rushed into the kitchen with Ruby. The side door slammed. Through the kitchen window, Hildy saw Mr. Farnham running toward his car.

Mrs. Farnham rolled herself out of the hallway into the kitchen. Both girls looked expectantly at her.

Her eyes were bright with tears, but she had a faint smile on her lips. "Matt's gone to get Connie. Her kidnapper promised we'd have her back within an hour!"

"Thank God!" Hildy breathed. "Oh, Mrs. Farnham, that's wonderful!"

Ruby asked, "Did ye git to talk to Connie this time?"

Mrs. Farnham shook her head, and tears sprang to her eyes again. She glanced at her son and pulled him close, but her eyes were on Hildy.

"Girls, please give Dickie and me a moment alone. Then, Ruby, you can do your usual dusting and cleaning, and Hildy, you can take Dickie outside and keep him busy. I'll want to be alone for a while."

The cousins nodded and walked in silence down the hallway into the spacious parlor. Hildy glanced at the antique grandfather clock standing majestically in the corner by the front door.

"Ten minutes to eight," she said thoughtfully.

"By nine, they ought to be home," Ruby mused. She paused, then added dolefully, "If'n she's ever a-comin' home!"

"Don't talk like that! She'll soon be here!"

The girls parted. Hildy took Dickie outside. She tried talking cheerfully to him, but her mind was elsewhere as the waiting began—again.

CHAPTER SEVENTEEN

A VITAL CLUE

Saturday and Sunday Morning

Hildy led Dickie to the back of the barn, where Spud was filling Robin's water trough.

Spud looked up at Hildy but didn't smile. "I heard the Pierce Arrow leave," he said. "I hope this time . . ." He stopped, his eyes dropping to the little boy. "Hey, Dickie," he continued, "want to see what I made for you this morning?"

Without waiting for an answer, Spud led the boy beyond the corral to the base of an ancient thorny locust near the southern fence line. Hildy followed.

"There," Spud said, pointing. "Your own sandbox! I also found you an old bucket and a garden trowel. Take off your shoes, and enjoy everything."

In spite of her concerns, Hildy smiled as the barefooted little boy sat in the sand pile and began digging.

"That was a very thoughtful thing to do, Spud," Hildy said with feeling.

"Kept me busy."

Hildy followed him to a nearby sycamore stump big enough for both of them to sit on. She asked, "Have you seen Brother Ben?"

"No. You?"

She shook her head, wishing she knew about the old Ranger's findings on the phone calls and wanting to share that information with Spud. Instead, she said, "I just wondered if he'd made any progress on finding a guardian for you."

"Don't need one! Soon as Connie's safely home, I'm hoboing to Chicago. You know that."

Hildy decided to drop the subject. She raised her voice. "What are you making, Dickie? A sand castle?"

He looked up and emptied a trowel of sand into the old galvanized bucket. "No," he said scornfully. "I'm digging a cave." He dumped the bucket off to one side.

Spud chuckled. "An imaginary cave in sand three inches deep."

Hildy wanted to talk to Spud about school and other problems, but she was more concerned about Connie.

The waiting dragged on. Dickie got tired of playing in the sand. Hildy placed him between Spud and herself and told him Bible stories. However, as the time inched by, her thoughts plunged into doubt about Connie's safety. *What's taking so long?*

Spud broke the silence. "Must be two hours now."

Hildy started to nod just as Dickie jumped up.

"Daddy's coming!" the boy shouted.

Hildy grabbed the little boy's hand and ran with Spud toward the garage.

As the Pierce Arrow approached, Hildy groaned aloud. "Oh, no! He's alone again!"

When the car stopped, Dickie ran forward. "Daddy, where's Connie?"

Mr. Farnham seemed so weary when he got out of the car that he could barely walk. He bent to pick up his son and held him tightly. The boy started to cry.

Hildy asked in a frightened, hushed voice, "What happened?"

The banker sounded incredibly sad. "I don't know. He didn't show up—again. I waited an extra hour . . ."

He was interrupted by his wife's heart-wrenching cry from

the open side door. He gripped his son tightly and ran toward her.

Hildy turned away, emotions swelling up inside and bursting forth from her mouth in angry words. "What kind of a person would do that twice to nice people like the Farnhams? And why?"

Ruby growled, "Wish I could git my hands on him fer five minutes! I'd l'arn him to hurt decent folks!"

Spud announced, "Here comes Ben."

Hildy blinked away her tears of frustration and led the run to meet the old Ranger. She blurted out the latest news as he got out of the Packard.

Ben nodded gravely. "I'm not surprised."

"What do you mean?" Hildy asked in bewilderment.

The old man looked down from his great height. "Because this reminds me of a case I had a long time ago when I was a U.S. marshal. And it ties in with what I've learned about the kidnapper so far."

Spud asked eagerly, "You've found something?"

Ben suggested, "Let's walk and talk."

They started moving slowly toward the back of the property. Ben asked Hildy if she'd told Spud and Ruby about the store and phones. She said she hadn't because he'd asked her not to say anything to anybody.

Ben nodded approval, then briefly told Spud and Ruby about the stolen food and Nellie Grimes' switchboard. Ben added, "The kidnapper's calls were made from that green phone booth outside Marden's store. When I questioned Stan Marden again this morning, he said a neighbor reported that some horse blankets and a lantern had been stolen from their barn a couple of weeks ago."

Ruby protested, "I ain't a follerin' ye a-tall!"

Hildy felt hope rise with her excitement.

Before she could explain to her cousin, Spud spoke up. "I do! The kidnapper needed the food, blankets, and lantern. The fact that he's phoning from the booth at the store ties in with the rest. He's hidden out close by!"

"Yup!" Ben said. "That's the way I figure it."

Spud turned to Hildy. "Maybe I'm wrong, and your hunch is right after all! He might be holding Connie down by the river. But how come nobody can find any trace of him down there?"

Hildy said, "I don't know, but we've got to go back down there and really look carefully. Remember what the kidnapper wrote in his note? If his conditions aren't met by noon tomorrow, we'll never see Connie again!"

Ruby protested, "That ain't our fault! Twice Mr. Farnham's done what the man said, but he didn't show up!"

Ben said softly, "I don't think he intended to show up."

Hildy felt suddenly sick inside. "Why not?"

"Revenge, Hildy," Ben answered softly. "Revenge."

Hildy couldn't believe her ears. "Just because Mrs. Farnham ran him off for using a pitchfork on Robin?"

"Has nothing to do with the horse," the old man said. "Stan Marden told me about this man who'd been in his store a month or so before. They got to talking. The stranger said his name was Myron Warmond."

Ruby asked, "Ye mean, that's the kidnapper's name?"

Hildy frowned. "Why would he give his name if he was planning a kidnapping? And revenge for what?"

Ben gave his moustache a flip. "I had a case years ago when the responsible—the guilty party—thought he was so smart he could give his name and still get away. His motive was revenge against a cattle company, but Myron Warmond seeks vengeance against banks. He focused on Lone River's banker as a way of getting even with all banks. Stan says that Warmond is bitter because he lost all his money when the banks failed and closed. He ended up drinking so hard he lost his wife and family. So he started drifting, blaming banks for his problems. In fact, Stan said this man praised John Dillinger and other bank robbers."

Everybody knew Dillinger's name. He was one of several bank robbers who had terrorized the Midwest during the Depression. The FBI had finally caught up with Dillinger in July and ended his outlaw career.

Hildy felt a new and more terrifying sense of danger for

Connie. "You mean, Brother Ben, that this Myron Warmond decided to take his revenge on Mr. Farnham just because he's a banker?"

"Yup! Understand, that's my theory based on past experience. Warmond didn't say a thing to Stan about the Farnhams. But one day when Warmond first came into the store, asking for a handout, he mentioned seeing the Lone River Bank. Stan said the owner lived down the road. Stan didn't think anything about it at the time."

"But why kidnap Connie?" Ruby demanded. "Why didn't this ol' kidnapper jist grab Mr. Farnham?"

Spud said, "I think I know why. Warmond wanted to hurt Mr. Farnham in the worst possible way. What's worse than kidnapping one of his children?"

"There's one thing that is worse," Ben said softly. "Never giving that child back."

Hildy gasped, "You think he's never going to return Connie? Never?"

Ben said grimly, "He used the phone calls to torment the Farnhams—raise their hopes, then dash them. I think, because of his deadline just twenty-five hours away, Warmond's going to call them one more time. But not for the ransom money. What he really wants is for the Farnhams to hurt as payment for his grudges."

Hildy turned away, her eyes blurring with sudden tears.

Ben said, "I persuaded that young sheriff's deputy to watch the phone booth. He thinks I'm just an old fool, but he's got no other leads, so he agreed. If Warmond makes the call from there, as I think he will, the deputy will follow him. Hopefully, that will lead to Connie."

Hildy regained her composure and walked on with the others. "But what if the kidnapper doesn't show up at the phone booth? Or what if he does and gets away from the deputy? Then the kidnapper could disappear forever, and we'd never find Connie. Oh, Brother Ben! We can't take that chance! We've got to find Connie ourselves—now!"

"But where'll we look?" Spud asked. "That river's been repeatedly searched by men, dogs, even us kids. Nobody's seen a trace of Connie."

Everyone fell silent as they passed under the locust tree by Dickie's sandbox. Hildy glanced at it, wondering if Connie would ever see it. Suddenly, she stopped.

"Wait!" Hildy exclaimed. "Now I know what's been bothering me about that man at the river! See Dickie's sandbox? Spud, remember when Dickie told us that he was digging a cave? And he emptied the sand out of his bucket? Ruby . . ."

"Buckets!" Ruby broke in. "You 'n' me seen that man empty two buckets of dirt in the river! Ye reckon he was a-diggin' a cave to hide Connie?"

Hildy nodded, excitement blazing in her eyes. "He didn't want any sign of dirt around where he'd been digging! That's what's been bothering me! I should have remembered it sooner!"

Ben frowned. "Couldn't be a cave. That would be in the side of the bluff or something. Too easy to spot. But a hole in the ground. . . !"

Hildy's voice rose in excitement. "He must have been preparing for the kidnapping when Ruby and I stumbled onto him! That's why he chased us and set his dog on us!"

Spud agreed. "That makes sense. By digging a pit and dumping the dirt in the river, there'd be no sign to show the hideout where he's keeping Connie. Everyone's been looking above ground for a tent or shack."

Ruby growled, "What're we a-waitin' fer? Let's go find him, dig him out, and save Connie!"

Ben held up both hands, palms outward to the trio. "Hold on! We can't go rushing off without a plan!"

"You have one?" Hildy asked hopefully.

"Yup! If Warmond follows his usual pattern—and most criminals do—he'll go back to the store to make his final call to Matt before the noon deadline. While he's doing that, we'll search for his hole in the ground."

"Won't he take Connie with him?" Hildy protested.

Ben shook his head. "I don't think so. My hunch is that he'll call Matt, tell him to bring the money to some remote spot, then say he'll tell where Connie is only after Matt hands over the ransom. Matt will do that, because his daughter means much more than the money."

Ruby asked, "But what if this kidnapper don't tell the truth about whar Connie really is? I think we ought to go a-lookin' fer her now!"

"Whoa," Ben said gently. "Let's think about it. I doubt the kidnapper will do anything until he gets the money from Matt. If we go down there now, he's likely to be laying low, just waiting for tomorrow.

"If he sees us, he might get suspicious and figure we're on to him. He could panic and do something terrible. I know it's hard to wait, but I really think we have no choice."

Reluctantly, Hildy, Spud, and Ruby agreed.

After dark, when Ben drove Hildy and Ruby up the lane to the barn-house, the Packard's headlights showed Nate Konning's Model T in the driveway.

Ruby exclaimed, "Muh daddy's back from Thunder Mountain! I wonder what he's decided about takin' that Ozark church!" She jumped out of the car and ran inside the barn-house.

Hildy said good night to the old Ranger, her mind still on Connie's terrible situation and with time almost gone. Still, it was important for Hildy to learn if her cousin and uncle were going to move away.

As Hildy stepped into the lamplight, Ruby whirled from her father. "Guess what, Hildy? We ain't a-gonna move to the Ozarks!"

Hildy felt a partial load of concern lifted from her shoulders. She gave Ruby a hug and said, "I'm glad!"

Nate Konning explained, "I feel God is calling me to minister to the people around Lone River."

Ruby leaned over and whispered in Hildy's ear, "I think the Widder Benton's got something to do with stayin' here!"

Hildy was sure her uncle would never put his personal feelings above what he felt was God's will, but Hildy didn't believe it was the time to tell Ruby that.

Her uncle said, "Tell me about Connie. Has she been found?"

The cousins reported the latest news. When the conversation died down, Hildy's uncle turned to her and changed the subject.

"I'm not given to listenin' to other folks' private talks, but I heard something mighty peculiar this afternoon. Since then, I've been arguing with myself whether telling you would be gossip and best kept to myself. But I've prayerfully considered it and decided it might help you understand something mighty important."

Hildy was suddenly very interested. "What is it?"

"I was powerful hongry—uh, hungry," her uncle began, "so I stopped at the bakery in town to git a doughnut. Nobody was in the place except me, and I guess the people arguing in the back room were talking so loud they didn't hear me. Now, I don't know Zelpha, but Ruby's told me about the way Zelpha's been treating you. I've met her daddy, who owns the bakery, so when I heard his voice and a girl talking real loud, I figured it was Zelpha."

"What were they saying?"

"Zelpha was sayin'—real loud—'This bakery means more to you than I do! You're never home. You never have time for me. And when you do talk to me, you're always criticizing and making me feel like I'm not worth any more to you than a sack of flour. No matter how hard I try, you never have one kind word to say! Well, I'll show you someday, Daddy! I'll find a way that'll make you see I'm special, and then you'll be sorry!' "

Nate paused, then asked hopefully, "Does that give you some idea of why Zelpha's always picking on you?"

"I understand some of it, Uncle Nate. After we find Connie, maybe I can figure it all out."

Hildy thought, *So that's why Zelpha got mad when I repeated something my daddy said. And maybe that's why she's trying so hard to get me disqualified from the scholarship. She's not really mad at me. She's mad at her father, but she's taking it out on me.*

Ordinarily, Hildy would have thought about that a lot more, but she'd been so concerned with Connie's danger that she hadn't been able to concentrate on the essay or the field trip to see the dirigible.

Ruby and her father had been gone only a little while when Hildy's father came home. She was surprised to see he wasn't wearing the arm sling. She resisted the temptation to ask about it until she'd told him the latest news about Connie, and Ben's plan for tomorrow.

Hildy's father reported on his visit to the doctor. "When ol' Doc Carson checked me today, he said I didn't need the sling anymore. Oh, I've got to be careful for a while, but at least I can join all of you in the search tomorrow morning."

"Oh, Daddy, I'm so glad! We'll all feel a lot safer with you there!"

———————

Shortly after dawn the next day, Hildy awoke with mixed feelings of dread and hope. She hated to miss Sunday school and church, but she told herself that if ever there was a time to do so, it was now. Finding Connie before the kidnapper's deadline was the most important thing in the world.

Hildy and her father picked up Ruby on the way to the mansion. There they met Spud. He said the kidnapper had not yet called, but Ben had. He wasn't feeling well, and was very sorry that he couldn't join the hunt. Hildy was concerned for the old Ranger, but she was more concerned about finding and rescuing Connie.

By eight o'clock, Hildy, her father, Ruby, and Spud headed for the river, with Lindy bounding along. After carefully looking to make sure the kidnapper wasn't in sight, the searchers waded across at the bend in the river where the stranger had disappeared.

Hildy whispered, "It's less than four hours to the deadline, but we don't have that long. If Ben's right, the kidnapper will be back in an hour or so. We've got to find Connie before then and get her to safety."

Hildy's father added, "You all know what to do. Keep a sharp eye out so the kidnapper doesn't sneak up on any of you! Okay, let's spread out and get started!"

Hildy nodded, thinking, *It's now or never!*

Chapter Eighteen

THE DANGEROUS SEARCH

Sunday

Hildy tried to still her anxious heart, but the dangerous task at hand made her jumpy. She focused her eyes on the ground, frequently glancing around to watch for the kidnapper and to make sure her father, Ruby, and Spud were close by.

But where is the kidnapper? Hildy wondered. *I sure hope he's at the store making the phone call to Mr. Farnham and not watching us. Wherever he is, we've got to find Connie before he gets back. Now, where would he most likely have dug that hole to keep her? It has got to be right around where he disappeared.*

Hildy comforted herself with the thought that the kidnapper's deadline was nearly four hours away, and he probably wouldn't return for at least an hour. That wasn't very much time, but it was all the four searchers had. So, in accordance with prearranged plans, Hildy, her father, Ruby, and Spud spread out with the dog and began slowly searching along the eastern river bank. The white bluff rose above and behind them. The cornfield started at the top of the bluff and stretched inland.

The dog seemed unconcerned, which indicated to Hildy that

the kidnapper probably wasn't around.

Hildy's heart beat faster as she carefully looked for signs that a man-made hole might be hidden under the fallen cottonwood leaves, small broken limbs, and twigs.

Periodically, Hildy checked to see where the others were. That wasn't easy, because the willows were taller and more dense now.

I don't like this! Hildy thought with a rising sense of concern. *We're getting separated! If I call out, the man might hear us. Connie might, too, but I can't take that risk!*

Hildy had passed the bluff at the bend in the river without seeing anything that might give a clue to Connie's whereabouts. Hildy turned around to go back, searching a few feet closer to the shore. She stepped over a fallen cottonwood log and began another sweep behind some dense willows.

She remembered having passed the butt end of the log a few minutes before. It had grown inland and fallen toward the water, breaking into four pieces. Three sections lay flat. Their blackened interiors clearly showed the hole that had helped kill and bring down the tree. The fourth piece, about two feet tall, stood on end. It was smaller around, indicating it had been near the top of the living tree.

Hildy had never seen any log fall that way. Curious, she stopped to examine it. The top was not hollow, but lightly covered with fallen leaves and debris. Hildy idly smacked the rough bark with her open right palm.

Whump! The stump made a hollow sound.

"Hmm!" Hildy exclaimed aloud, still only mildly curious. She glanced at the debris-strewn top. "Maybe it's only partly hollow." She rose and started to resume her search.

Suddenly she knelt and gave the piece of log another smack with her open palm.

Whump! She heard the same hollow sound.

Her curiosity rising, Hildy brushed fallen cottonwood and willow leaves off the top. It was surprisingly flat, not uneven and jagged as happens when a tree falls of itself, twisting and snapping off ragged pieces.

Suddenly, Hildy stopped brushing. The top of the log, free

of debris, was covered with a gunny sack. She pulled it aside and stared in surprise.

It is hollow—with something sticking up! Looks like a piece of rusted stovepipe! She gingerly touched it. *It is stovepipe! But why?*

In her excitement to get a better look, Hildy swung her body around. Repositioning her feet caused another thumping sound directly under her feet.

Hildy dropped to her knees and swiftly brushed the dirt and leaves away around her feet. Seconds later, she stopped. *Boards!*

Breathing hard with excitement, she finished sweeping the debris away until the boards were fully exposed. Closely nailed together, they covered an area about six feet long and four feet wide.

"This is it!" Hildy whispered aloud. She raised up and glanced around. There was nobody in sight. She thought of jumping up to run tell the others, then looked back at the stovepipe.

Could that be for fresh air? Excitedly, Hildy bent over the open top of the rusted metal pipe. *Yes! That's what it is! It brings fresh air to the pit below. It will probably also carry sound.* Hildy put her mouth close to the open end of pipe and called softly, "Connie?"

She turned her face away, placing her right ear close to the pipe. Through it, Hildy heard a tiny, weak, and frightened sob.

Hildy wanted to shout with joy, but she forced herself to keep her voice down while again speaking into the stovepipe. "Connie, it's Hildy. I'm going to get you out. Hang on! I've got to find the way into this place!"

For a moment Hildy debated about whether to run and tell the others or try finding the entrance to the underground prison. Then she decided. *Can't take the time! Got to get her out now!*

Hildy ran her hands frantically along the edges of the boards. Sand scoured her fingertips, and splinters pricked her fingers, but she kept feeling.

Suddenly she stopped dead still at the sound of a footstep behind her. She whirled around, heart racing and hands upraised to defend herself.

Ruby cried hoarsely, "Hey! It's me!"

Hildy took a deep breath and tried to swallow the lump of fear in her throat. "I've found Connie!" she exclaimed in a whisper. She pointed to the boards. "Help me find the entrance!"

The girls dropped to their knees and swept their hands back and forth over the exposed boards, particularly the edges. Hildy kept glancing up, her heart still racing, fearful the kidnapper would emerge from the willows. They were so close to the river that he could be upon them if they didn't see him first. They couldn't expect to hear him coming above the sounds of the fast-moving, shallow water.

Connie started making muffled, frightened sounds from beneath the cousins' feet. Both whispered hoarse reassurances while frantically digging.

Ruby suddenly whispered, "Here!"

Hildy spun around, the sand on the boards grating under her shoes. She dropped to both knees beside her cousin.

Ruby was starting to pull back a square section of boards at the corner nearest the river. Hildy joined her, working fast. The girls slowly got the loose end tilted up. Sand fell back, exposing two rusty hinges.

Hildy held on to the top edge of the door and lowered her head even with the ground. "Connie? I can't see! Where are you?"

"Back here!" The voice was tiny and weak.

"Where?" Hildy asked, peering into the dark hole. It smelled of moist earth, stale air, and kerosene. Light filtering over Hildy's shoulder showed that the walls were lined with old boards to keep them from caving in.

For a moment that was all Hildy saw. Then she caught a movement at the far end, where it was darkest.

"I see her!" Hildy exclaimed. "Hold this open. I'm going in after her."

As Hildy lowered herself feet-first into the hole, Ruby hissed a warning. "Ye better hurry! No tellin' when he might come back!"

"I'm hurrying!" Hildy dropped to her hands and knees while her eyes adjusted from the bright sunshine outside to the damp gloom of the hole. Hildy's body blocked the outside light, but she reached forward.

"It's all right, Connie, " Hildy said reassuringly. "Let me have your hand!" She felt around and touched a kerosene lantern. It fell over. Hildy instinctively drew back, her feet banging noisily into an empty bucket.

Ruby whispered from behind her, "Ye tryin' to wake the daid?"

Hildy ignored her cousin's frightened voice. "Connie," she called, her words echoing in the wooden pit. "I can't see you! Give me your hand!"

"I can't!"

"Sure you can!" Hildy kept reaching but touched nothing. Then a realization hit her. "Are you tied up?"

"Uh-huh."

Hildy felt in the gloom until she touched something rough. She recognized it as a horse blanket. She kept feeling until her fingers touched bare feet, then ropes. Hildy's bleeding fingers moved up to feel the little girl's hands, tied with ropes at the wrists.

"I'll get you outside," Hildy said, gripping Connie's underarms. "Then we'll untie you. Now, don't be scared. Here we go!"

It was necessary to turn the little girl around and drag her backward. Hildy bent double, her shoulders and back touching the wooden roof. She shuffled toward the light, continuing a steady stream of reassuring words to the captive.

"That man . . ." Connie began.

"Don't talk!" Hildy pulled hard, aware of the gritty sand underfoot and the possibility of splinters from the rough plank floor. But she kept pulling, moving backward in haste. "He can't scare you anymore!" To herself, Hildy added, *I hope*!

Hildy inched toward the circle of light where Ruby waited at the entrance.

Connie began trembling violently.

Ruby leaned down so her head was inside the entry. "She all right?"

"I think so. Here, grab her shoulders and hold on until I can get underneath her and push. Then slide your hands under her armpits. Ready?"

"Ready!"

Hildy released her grip as Ruby clutched Connie's dress just above both shoulders. Hildy dropped to the sandy floor and wrapped her arms around the little girl's thighs. "Lift!" Hildy puffed, doing the same herself.

For such a little girl, Connie was amazingly awkward to get through the small doorway.

With a final push and pull, Connie was through the hole. Ruby fell backward into the willows with the bound girl sprawling awkwardly on top. Hildy scrambled out into the daylight. Connie hunched up, her shoulders protecting her closed eyes from the sudden change of darkness to sunlight.

"Untie her feet!" Hildy instructed, glancing around in hopes of seeing her father or Spud. "I'll get her hands!"

"She's barefooted, an' they's no time to go back in thar a-lookin' fer her shoes!" Ruby freed the girl's ankles first. "Thar!" she said, straightening up. "Hurry up!"

"I'm trying, but this knot's tight!"

Ruby looked around, then leaned over Hildy and Connie. "I shore feel a lot better, knowin' how he disappeared into this here hole. I'm shore glad he ain't no haint!"

"Talk later!" Hildy urged. "He may be back any second! There, it's off! Connie, can you stand up?"

"I think so." She tried but fell back.

"Her legs are cramped from being tied up," Hildy said. "We'll have to carry her." Hildy knelt to lift the child into her arms.

Ruby warned, "Gonna be mighty hard fer you 'n me to do that an' hurry at the same time!" She glanced around again. "Now whar'd yore daddy and Spud git to?"

"We can't wait!" Hildy puffed, standing with difficulty, the girl in her arms. "Head for the river!"

Connie's face was smudged from tears that had made muddy streaks down her cheeks. Her hair was a rat's nest, and her clothes were filthy. She was still trembling and blinking her eyes as they adjusted to the sunlight.

"I'm—scared!" her words came out barely audible. "That man . . ."

Ruby interrupted. "Stop a-thinkin' about him."

Hildy started walking. "Ruby, go find Daddy and Spud. Don't yell! The kidnapper might hear you. Meet us by the crossing."

Ruby nodded, pushed through the willows, and disappeared.

Hildy turned toward the river, still carrying Connie in her arms. Because Hildy's hands weren't free to hold the lithe willows aside as she plunged through them, the slender branches sprang back like switches to deliver stinging pain to her face and bare arms.

Connie sure is heavy! I hope Daddy gets here fast! But I don't know how far he can carry her with his sore arm!

Hildy was puffing hard and staggering, even on the downhill slant toward the river. "Connie," she panted, "when we get to the water, I'm going to have to put you down a minute. If you can stand by then, we'll wade across the river. Daddy and Spud'll be along and . . ."

A movement upstream caught Hildy's eye. She stopped abruptly in the middle of the last clump of willows on the riverbank. "Shh!" she hissed.

"It's him!" Connie whimpered. "I see him!"

Hildy hugged the little girl tightly and breathed a warning. "Don't move!"

The man waded downstream as before, the noise of the shallow river covering any sound of his coming. He carried the same three-pointed spear.

Hildy's heart thudded so hard she thought it would burst through her chest. Beneath her left hand, she could feel Connie's chest heaving in frightened convulsions.

The kidnapper turned toward shore and waded directly toward the hidden girls.

Connie whimpered in fear, "He's going to get us!"

——

CHAPTER NINETEEN

A RUN FOR LIFE

Sunday

Connie repeated fearfully, "He's going to get us!"

"Shh!" Hildy lightly clamped her hand over Connie's mouth, hoping the kidnapper wouldn't hear them above the sound of rushing water. "Stay down!"

Hildy tried to crouch down more, but Connie's weight threw her off balance. She fell hard on her backside but managed to keep her hold on the little girl.

Hildy glanced up in alarm at the willows dancing wildly overhead. She was sure the kidnapper would see them, but he suddenly looked down and halfheartedly struck at the wake of a passing salmon with the spear. Then he continued straight toward the hidden girls.

He's going to walk right over us! Hildy's mind screamed.

It took all her willpower to remain motionless, her hand across Connie's mouth. The kidnapper was within six feet of the frightened girls when he turned slightly to avoid a dense growth of willows leaning from the bank. He pushed them back with the spear handle, waded out of the river, and crossed the gravel bar toward his hideout.

Hildy let out a long, shuddering breath and whispered in

Connie's ear. "I'm going to take my hand off your mouth, but don't make any noise!"

Connie nodded. Hildy released her. Cautiously, Hildy rose to a half crouch, looking through the willows for some sign of her father, Ruby, or Spud.

Nowhere in sight! Well, I can't wait!

Stooping again, Hildy whispered, "We've got to get as far away as possible before the man discovers you're gone. I'll have to carry you again."

This time it was more difficult to lift Connie. She seemed heavier, and Hildy hurt from the many bleeding cuts and scrapes to which sand and dry leaves stuck.

With a grunt, Hildy got to her feet. Connie locked her arms around Hildy's neck, so it was easier to whisper in the little girl's ear. "When he finds you're gone, he'll come looking. But don't be scared! Daddy and Spud will be along soon, so we'll be okay—especially if we can get across the river first."

With another quick look to be sure the kidnapper was out of sight, Hildy stepped out of the sheltering willows and waded into the river.

The stream seemed much stronger and swifter, but Hildy realized it was really the little girl's weight that made walking difficult. Hildy started to stumble, regained her balance, and kept going.

About a third of the way across, after almost falling again, Hildy stopped, breathing hard, to look back. Nothing moved. There was no sign of anybody.

Wonder where Daddy, Ruby, and Spud are? Hope they didn't run into that man! I couldn't hear them over the sound of this water.

Aloud, she announced with forced cheerfulness, "It's okay so far, Connie! I've got to catch my breath, so I'm going to put you down. But don't worry! The water won't come to much above your waist, and I'll hang on to you."

Connie nodded bravely, but the river's strength swept her off-balance. She squealed in fright. Hildy snatched her up again, struggling to keep the frightened child from choking her.

"Not so tight!" Hildy cried hoarsely, starting forward again. "You'll be all right!"

Connie whimpered, her body shaking, as Hildy tried to see around the child's head. Hildy picked as smooth a path as possible through the hundreds of rounded rocks clearly visible at the bottom.

As Hildy waded out farther, the stronger, faster current combined with slippery rocks to make her every step more precarious. Hildy's foot skidded on a rock. She started to fall forward, regained her footing, and straightened up, with Connie's face inches from the water.

Hildy's heart was pumping furiously, and her breathing was labored when she reached midstream. She stopped momentarily to risk a look back. There was no sign of the kidnapper.

He's got to know Connie's gone, so he must be out of the hole by now and looking for her. So why can't I see him?

Hildy caught a flash of movement on top of the bluff. *That was Daddy! Oh, no! He's going into the cornfield! Where're Ruby and Spud?*

Hildy dropped her gaze to sweep the area below the corn. The willows moved to her right.

"There's Spud! See him, Connie? He's running this way. But where's Lindy? Oh, there he is—away off by himself! Here he comes!"

Lindy bounded out of the willows about a hundred yards upstream, away from the hideout, and plunged into the water. He swam strongly toward Hildy and Connie.

Ruby broke into the open behind Spud and ran after him. Ruby kept glancing back and to both sides, obviously looking for Hildy's father.

Hildy held Connie with her left arm and waved frantically with her right, signaling her location in the river. She wanted to shout, but didn't dare. She sighed with relief as Spud and Ruby waved back. Then Hildy pointed toward where the kidnapper had disappeared and frantically jabbed her free hand toward the hole where she'd found Connie.

Hildy wanted to shout, "He's over there!" but she could only mouth the words and hope Spud and Ruby understood and would stay alert to the danger.

Aloud, Hildy said, "They're coming! See? Ruby and Spud are coming!" She hugged the trembling little girl closer. It's going to be all right!"

Hildy started wading again, feeling the water rise above her knees. "Just a little farther, Connie!"

Hurrying made the slippery rocks beneath Hildy's feet more treacherous, but she didn't dare slow up. Risking another look back to see if the kidnapper was after them, she slipped on a slick rock and fell forward. "Hang on!" she managed to cry just before both girls plunged face first into the water.

Hildy couldn't swim, but managed to hang on to Connie with one hand while struggling to regain her feet. She came up gasping. She pulled Connie to her feet, coughing and choking, but she didn't try to pick her up again.

"It's okay!" Hildy said, fighting her own feeling of gagging on water she'd swallowed. "We're almost there! It's shallow, and I'll hold your hand. You can make it the rest of the way!"

A few steps more and both girls crawled ashore on their hands and knees. They sprawled on the sand, too weak to speak. Hildy's lungs burned, and her heart pounded as she clutched the soaking-wet child tightly in her arms.

Hildy sucked in ragged gulps of air through her mouth. "We made it! And here comes Spud and Ruby! But where's Daddy— and the tramp?"

Connie drew back at sight of the charging dog. Hildy said quickly, "He won't hurt you! That's Lindy. He likes little girls. You can pet him."

Hildy demonstrated by reaching out to the wet dog. Cautiously, Connie did the same.

Hildy's eyes flickered across the cornfield at the top of the bluff. "There! That's my daddy!" She let go of Connie and stood up to wave both hands wildly above her head. "He sees us! He's waving back!"

Hildy was still trying to catch her breath when Ruby and Spud staggered across the small stretch of sand to where Hildy, Connie, and Lindy waited.

"Let's get out of here!" Spud exclaimed, looking anxiously

across the river. "I saw him, but he didn't see me—Warmond, the kidnapper! He'll be after us with that spear!"

Hildy protested, "We can't leave Daddy!"

"He'll be all right!" Spud said sternly. "Besides, there's no time to spare!" He knelt in front of Connie and turned his back to her. "I'll carry her now."

Hildy nodded, still too winded to talk. She looked across to the top of the bluff and the cornfield. There was no sign of her father now. A horrible thought hit her. *What if the kidnapper caught Daddy? With his sore arm . . .*

Spud's urgent tone interrupted Hildy's thoughts.

"Let's go!" Spud commanded. "Help get her on my back. She'll be easier to carry that way."

Hildy and Ruby obeyed, and Spud stood upright with some difficulty. Carrying Connie piggyback, he started jogging inland toward the oaks and the mansion beyond. Ruby was a few steps behind.

Hildy started to follow, then glanced back again. "The kidnapper's coming! With his spear!"

Ruby called over her shoulder, "Don't jist stand thar a-lookin'! Run!"

"I don't see my daddy! He may not know the man's there, and Daddy's arm . . ."

"He kin take keer of hisself!" Ruby called. "But if'n that man ketches us . . ."

Hildy didn't hear the rest. She saw Warmond wade into the river, yelling. She couldn't understand him above the river's noise, but she could guess from the furious look on his face that he was cursing or saying terrible things.

Hildy turned and ran after the others. She quickly caught up with Spud. He was trying valiantly, but his ruddy face was already flushed from the hard work of carrying a thirty-pound weight on his back while running across uneven ground, around fallen logs, stumps and rocks.

"Let me carry her awhile!" Hildy suggested.

Spud shook his head, panting too hard to waste time with words. Lindy ran beside him.

Ruby said, "I'm strong's a boy! Lemme spell ye!"

Again, Spud shook his head and kept running. He staggered, caught himself, and regained his balance as Lindy bounded out of the way.

Spud glanced at Hildy, gasping hoarsely. "I can keep going until your father gets here. Or maybe when Warmond knows your father's behind him, he'll quit chasing us!"

Hildy looked back in alarm. "He might turn on Daddy, and Daddy's got a sore arm! The man's got a spear!"

She caught a glimpse of her father running across the gravel bar on the far shore. He was too far away to hear a shouted warning. He was well behind the kidnapper, who was splashing out of the river on the near shore.

"Too late!" Hildy groaned in despair. "He's coming so fast he'll be on us before Daddy can catch up to him!"

For another second, Hildy stood looking back and trying to catch her breath. She was surprised at how fast the kidnapper could run, even with the spear. He had already covered about twenty feet from the shallow river.

On the far shore Hildy saw her father run into the river, throwing up spray from the speed of his efforts. His mouth was moving, and Hildy guessed he was shouting at the stranger.

The kidnapper didn't seem to realize that Joe Corrigan was behind him. Hildy guessed that either the noise of the rushing river drowned out her father's shouting, or the kidnapper was concentrating so hard on catching the fugitives that he wasn't aware he was also being pursued.

Hildy turned and raced after the others. "Daddy can't get here before the tramp catches us!" she shouted. "We'd better split up!"

"No, not yet!" Spud exclaimed, slowing and swinging around with Connie still riding piggyback. "Lindy!"

The Airedale cocked his ears and looked up, tongue rolling heavily from his open mouth.

"Sic him!" Spud commanded, swinging his right arm in a sweeping motion toward the oncoming kidnapper.

With a sharp bark, the dog obeyed.

"No!" Hildy cried in alarm. "That wasn't in the plan! He could get killed! Call him back!"

Spud gave Connie a quick hitch higher up on his back and started running away. "Lindy's too smart to get close to that spear, but he'll delay that guy! Come on!"

Hildy and Ruby looked at each other doubtfully as the dog bounded toward the kidnapper, barking furiously.

The stranger stopped and pointed the three-pointed spear toward the dog. Instantly, Lindy bounded aside, well beyond the dangerous weapon. The dog slid to a halt, stopped barking, and lowered his head. He began a slow, menacing advance toward the kidnapper.

Hildy watched in frightened fascination as the man began jabbing the spear at the dog. Lindy leaped aside, growling menacingly. The dog circled to his left and out of sight behind a large downed cottonwood log.

From behind her, Hildy heard Spud yell for the girls to come on.

She glanced at her father. He was halfway across the river.

I don't think the kidnapper knows Daddy's coming! If Lindy can just keep the man there for another minute or two . . .

Hildy saw her father suddenly stumble, try to catch himself, then pitch forward. He tried to break his fall with outflung hands, but his head and shoulders disappeared under the water.

"Daddy!" she shrieked, knowing he couldn't swim.

Joe Corrigan exploded upward, regained his feet in the shallow water and continued wading rapidly toward shore, while his cowboy hat floated downstream.

Hildy gave a big sigh of relief. At the same instant, out of the corner of her eye, she saw the stranger suddenly draw back his right arm, aiming the spear at the Airedale.

"Lindy, look out!" she screamed.

Sunlight reflected off the three points as the weapon sailed through the air. The tines smashed downward and disappeared behind the log. She heard it strike, followed by a single yelp from the dog. Then silence.

"Oh, Lindy!" Hildy cried, her voice breaking. She turned

away, glad that Spud had not seen what had just happened. He was running, his back to Hildy, panting so loudly he had not heard Lindy's yelp of pain.

The kidnapper gave a triumphant yell, rushed around the end of the log and straight for the girls. But there was no sign or sound from Lindy.

"Run!" Hildy cried, turning with her cousin to race after Spud. "Split up! Ruby, you run that way!" She pointed to the right. "I'll go this way! He can't chase all of us! If he chases after Spud and Connie, let's you and I turn back and help them! Daddy'll be here in a minute!"

Hildy darted off toward a huge tangle of wild blackberry vines higher than her head and parallel to the river. She glanced around to make sure that Spud was still running straight toward the mansion, carrying Connie piggyback.

Winded but scared enough to keep running along the blackberry vines, Hildy hurt inside because of Lindy and wondered how close her father was. He was a strong man, and he would be plenty mad at anyone who was chasing his daughter. Hildy didn't want to think about what her father would do, even with a bad arm, when he caught up to the kidnapper.

She stopped to look back and catch her breath. Spud and Connie were still heading toward the mansion, although Spud was stumbling and slowed almost to a walk.

Behind him and well off to the far side, Ruby was still running.

But where's the stranger? And Daddy? There had been time enough for the man to come into sight, chasing hard after one of them. But he was nowhere to be seen.

Where'd he go? Hildy wondered, nearing the far end of the blackberry vines. She slowed, stopped and looked back. *There's Ruby, and Spud with Connie. Oh, Daddy must have caught up with him behind these vines!*

Then Hildy heard a sound behind her. She whirled around, but it was too late.

With an angry roar like a wild animal, the kidnapper leaped

from behind the end of the blackberry vines. He clamped both arms around Hildy's, pinning them to her sides.

Through clenched teeth he grated harshly, "Now, you little troublemaker, you're going to pay!"

CHAPTER TWENTY

UP, UP INTO THE SKY

Sunday Morning and Later

Hildy struggled against the powerful arms pinning down her own. "Let—me—go!"

The kidnapper laughed, but with no humor. His raspy voice came through broken yellow teeth. "From the first minute I saw you, I knew you were trouble! Well, you may have saved your little sister—or whoever she was—but you're going to more than make up for what it cost me to lose her!"

He lifted the helpless Hildy off the ground and started to turn around with her crushed against his chest. Then he let out a scream of pain and dropped her.

Hildy sprawled backward, landing almost flat on her back. One bare arm raked along a thorny blackberry vine, but Hildy was too dazed to notice the pain.

She heard a low growl and fearsome snarls, followed by another shriek of pain.

Hildy sat up to see a small brown tornado of a dog flashing in and out, snapping at the kidnapper's pant legs and ripping them to shreds.

"Lindy!" Hildy cried. "Oh, Lindy! You're okay!"

The dog didn't seem to hear. His broad head had a bloody

gash, but he was still strong and fast. He leaped again and again at the stranger's legs. Wide open jaws with fearsome teeth snapped. Lindy leaped away with a mouthful of shredded overall pants.

Then, darting in again, the dog avoided the man's outthrust hands and clumsy kicks. Lindy leaped up, great jaws clicking sharply together above the man's heavy leather boots.

The tramp screeched in mortal fear, stumbling backward in a mindless effort to escape. "Get him off me!" he screamed, trying to break the dog's repeated short charges with his bare hands, then jerking them back as the flashing jaws snapped at them.

Hildy got unsteadily to her feet, tears leaping unbidden to her eyes. "Oh, Lindy! Lindy!"

The dog jumped to one side, spun fast as a rattler striking, and bore in again, leaping toward the unprotected legs above the man's boots.

The tramp backed against the sharp thorns of the berry bush and leaped away from them with another howl of pain. Then he made a choice. He twisted sideways and started scrambling up the high vines, pulling himself up with bare hands on vines carrying half-inch thorns.

Once more, Lindy jumped high, fangs bared. They snapped down on the man's hip pocket and ripped it away. This time, the dog seemed to have bitten more than the overalls, for Hildy again heard a scream of pain from the kidnapper.

It all happened so fast that Hildy didn't hear or see anything else until her father's voice sounded nearby.

"You okay, Hildy?"

She turned as he rushed around the corner of the blackberry vines. "Oh, Daddy!" she cried, letting him take her into his arms.

Hildy's eyes lifted again to the kidnapper. He had scrambled to the top of a high tangle of vicious blackberry vines. There he squawked wildly for help, while Lindy kept leaping, trying for one more bite.

Hildy shifted her gaze. Ruby had changed directions and was

now running toward Hildy and her father. Off to the right, Spud had eased Connie to the ground and knelt down.

Spud was too winded to whistle, but he managed to puff out a command. "Lindy! Here, boy!"

The Airedale turned and ran joyously, tongue rolling, until he bounded into Spud's open arms.

Hildy was shaking from a combination of excitement and relief when she answered her father's question. "Oh, yes, Daddy, I'm fine! In fact, everything's just fine!"

"Good!" he replied. "Now I'd better get that fellow down from those blackberry vines before there's nothing left to put in jail."

———

That night, unable to sleep as she thought of the day's events, Hildy lay in the darkened barn-house and remembered she still had big problems at school.

She'd forgotten them for a while after the dramatic rescue, chase, and capture along the river. For hours after that, everything had been a happy blur of glad shouts, happy tears, and loud words of praise.

Now that was past, and the future was upon Hildy.

She thought of Zelpha, Miss Krutz, the scholarship, and the upcoming trip to see the dirigible. Hildy folded her hands across her chest and looked up at the barn rafters, invisible in the darkness.

I thank Thee for all the good things that have happened: for Connie being safe, her kidnapper in jail, Ruby not moving away, and Daddy finding a house where I won't have to change schools, and Brother Ben being fine again. I guess I don't have a right to ask for anything more, but, well, I'd really like to win that scholarship. I'd like to smooth things over with Zelpha, and I don't want Spud to move away.

Hildy's thoughts jumped. *"This one thing I do . . ."*

It's not over, Hildy told herself. *As exciting as things have been, it's still not over. But now what?*

———

The next morning Hildy was surprised at the change of attitude when she got on the bus. Mr. Henderson, the driver, smiled and said, "Great job, Hildy!" Other kids who'd ignored her before reached out to touch her and say something nice as she made her way to sit beside Ruby.

"Ain't nary a soul in Lone River that's not heerd about yestiddy," Ruby said with a wide grin. "They know ever'thing, includin' how the dep'ity got anxious waiting at the phone booth and followed the tramp, but he got away. Or he would've if it hadn't been fer us! So ever'body likes us all of a sudden— 'ceptin' Zelpha."

Hildy glanced at Zelpha, who remained in her seat, staring out the window, ignoring everyone. She turned briefly and caught Hildy's eye. Hildy had never seen such terrible, naked hatred—and something else. Hildy couldn't be sure what it was, but it worried her.

At the school grounds, Hildy noticed that Edna and Tessie didn't meet Zelpha as they always had. Instead, Zelpha made her solitary way toward the school, while other students who'd heard about the rescue clustered around Hildy and Ruby.

Hildy pushed her way free of the mob and caught up with Zelpha. "Look," Hildy began, "I've been thinking a lot lately. I'm sorry about your problems with your father, but that's no reason to take your anger out on me."

Zelpha faced Hildy with angry eyes. "You're a big heroine right now, you and your Okie cousin! But you haven't changed one bit in my eyes! You're still nothing! I'm somebody, and that's the way it's always going to be. You'll see. And so will . . ." She bit off the sentence, then added, "Now get away from me and stay away!"

As Hildy and Ruby entered the building, the principal was waiting for them. "I owe you both an apology," he began with a big smile of welcome. "I hope we can forget all about our first meeting a week ago."

"It's forgotten," Hildy assured him, and Ruby nodded. The girls went on to their homeroom.

Miss Krutz got up from her desk and met the girls, taking

each by the hand. "I have been wrong, at least on some things, as on Friday," she said.

Hildy knew the teacher still held the note incidents against her. Hildy wished Miss Krutz knew the truth about that, but Hildy couldn't tell her.

The teacher added simply, "I am proud to have you both as my students."

The change in attitude continued throughout the week, except for Zelpha. She remained aloof, sullen, and withdrawn, giving Hildy an uneasy feeling.

On Saturday when Hildy boarded the bus for the field trip to see the dirigible, she was relieved that Zelpha was not along. Tessie and Edna treated Hildy and Ruby in the same friendly fashion as everyone else.

Hildy wondered why Zelpha hadn't been on the bus, but that was forgotten as the cousins disembarked outside the Sunnyvale Naval Air Station. There was a stirring of excitement about seeing the great dirigible when it arrived shortly for mooring.

"There's Spud!" Hildy said, waving as he got out of Brother Ben's yellow Packard. "I'm glad he—I mean, they—could come."

Ruby's attitude toward Spud had softened somewhat since his heroic piggyback run with Connie, but Ruby was not one to change totally. She said, "Hildy, ye may's well go talk to him by yoreself. I'll meet ye down front with the rest of our class." She hurried away.

Hildy walked up to Spud and the old Ranger.

"Greetings and felicitations!" Spud said with a grin. "Ben and I decided to drive over and see the dirigible landing. He's never seen one."

Ben Strong grabbed his white cowboy hat as a gust of wind whirled by, making Hildy's skirt dance.

"Whoops!" she said, holding it down. "That sort of sneaked up on us."

Ben resettled his hat on his head. "I heard on the radio this morning that there's a storm coming. They're expecting snow in the mountains. A lot of deer hunters are likely to get caught up there."

Hildy glanced at the sky. It was clear and blue, a beautiful autumn day. "You don't think it's going to stop the landing, do you?"

"Not unless the wind whips up more than this," Ben replied. He turned to Spud. "Don't you have some news for Hildy?"

Spud took off his aviator cap, letting the breeze ruffle his reddish hair. "I don't quite know how to say it," he began, looking at his big hands.

"Say what?" Hildy asked, suddenly concerned that he might be leaving for Chicago.

"Well," Spud said, "Ben helped Matthew Farnham write a letter to my ol' man—uh, my father . . ."

"Your father?" Hildy broke in.

Spud nodded. "Mr. Farnham wants to know if he can be my guardian so I can stay here and go to school."

"Oh, Spud!" Hildy clapped her hands together and jumped up and down. "That's wonderful!"

The old Ranger grinned and gave his moustache a flip with the back of his right forefinger. "I can see you're not very excited about that, Hildy!"

She felt herself flush with embarrassment. "Guess I didn't respond in a very ladylike way," she admitted.

Spud said, "Forget it! I like the Farnhams, and they seem to like me. Besides, they need somebody around the house, and Lindy and I have both been welcome."

With Spud on one side and Brother Ben on the other, Hildy wanted to skip with joy as she was escorted toward the gates. Then she stopped. "I see a drinking fountain. You go ahead. I'll catch up with you."

She pushed through the crowd to the fountain and bent to take a drink. When she heard Zelpha's voice, Hildy raised up, scanning a row of cars parked about thirty feet away. Hildy recognized the back of Zelpha's head, with her aunt standing beside her. Both were facing a man Hildy had never seen before.

Zelpha cried, "Oh, Daddy, please stop! You're going to make Aunt Poppy cry again!"

So that's Zelpha's father, Hildy thought.

The man snapped, "I'm losing patience with both of you!"

Zelpha exclaimed, "Daddy, please try to understand. Aunt Poppy and I have always tried to do everything you ask. But all you've done on the ride over here is . . ."

"That's enough, young lady!"

Zelpha's voice rose sharply. "Someday you'll go too far, Daddy!"

"Zelpha's right!" Miss Krutz's tone was abrupt. "Someday you'll go too far, Karl!"

"Don't threaten me, Poppy! You owe your job to me. So does Ebenezer Wiley and everyone else at that school."

"Well," Zelpha snapped, "I don't work for you! But I am sorry to be such a disappointment to you! Someday I'll show you! I'll find a way to make you see . . ." She broke off in a sob and ran across the parking lot toward the grandstand.

A few minutes later, Hildy pushed through the crowd of adults and students who had taken seats in the bleachers to await the dirigible's arrival.

"Over here!" Spud called, waving.

Hildy saw that he, Brother Ben, and the Farnhams had all found seats in the second row from the front. Mrs. Farnham had been lifted out of her wheelchair so she could sit at the far end of the row. The empty chair was beside her in the aisle. Dickie sat between his mother and father. Connie was on his right with Spud next to her. Then came Edna and Ruby with Tessie on the far right. Ruby was talking to Edna and Tessie as though they'd never been anything but friends.

Hildy made her way past other spectators in the second row and started to sit down between Spud and Connie. Hildy reached out to put her arms around the little girl and accidentally brushed the back of the person in front of her. "Oh, I'm sorry," she apologized.

Zelpha Krutz turned around, gave Hildy an icy glare, then wordlessly swung back to face the mooring field.

Hildy thought, *Brrr! It's cold here, and not just from that wind blowing in off the ocean.*

"Here it comes!" Connie shouted, jumping up beside Hildy and pointing. "Here it comes!"

There was a collective gasp from the audience as the great airship eased over the coastal hills into full view. It came slowly toward them, the distinctive sound of the motors replacing the crowd's exclamations. They slipped into an awed silence.

The motors were not high and angry-sounding like airplanes Hildy had often heard. Instead, the dirigible power plants made such a low-pitched noise they seemed to rumble like distant thunder. The result was a slow, audible vibration that seemed to be felt as much as heard. Hildy had an unforgettable sense of the tremendous power necessary to lift the huge aircraft from the earth.

Hildy was speechless. She had seen the dirigible over the barn-house, but it had been much higher in the sky. This time it was much lower, and heading lower still.

Countless sailors as line handlers were on the field, positioned so they would be on either side of the immense aircraft when it nosed into the mooring mast.

Hildy saw a gust of wind catch the sailors' bell-bottom trousers and make them snap smartly. Then the breeze passed, and Hildy looked up again as the massive dirigible slowly eased into position.

The cables dropped from both sides of the ship, and line handlers grabbed them. They braced themselves to start pulling upon command.

A sudden gust of wind whirled over the grandstand. At the same instant, the immense airship lurched slightly upward. Hildy's hand flew to her mouth. The collective spectators gave a gasp that sounded as though it came from one throat.

The dirigible surged sideways, toward the crowd. The sailors leaned backward, bracing themselves and desperately holding on to the cables. The wind was too strong. The line handlers were dragged across the pavement. Hildy joined the crowd that instinctively drew back from the incredible spectacle.

The massive shadow cast by the monstrous airship fell across Hildy and the crowd. Some sailors let go their lines. These trailed loosely like living things, twisting in the wind.

Suddenly, Zelpha jumped up right in front of Hildy. "I'll help!" Zelpha cried, rushing toward a cable.

"Zelpha, no!" Hildy cried.

It was too late. Zelpha leaped up, caught a line, and held on as the wind continued to sweep the airship sideways toward the crowd. Suddenly, the dirigible started to rise. Hildy saw Zelpha's feet leave the ground.

Hildy didn't think. She just acted. She leaped up, dashed the short distance to where Zelpha hung, and jumped up, grabbing on to the heavy cable.

"Let go!" Hildy cried, looking into the frightened face inches from her own. "Let go now!"

Hildy felt someone leap up behind her. She saw strong hands clamped on the line just above her own. She thought they belonged to another sailor until she heard the voice.

"Let go, Hildy!" Spud yelled. "Zelpha, you too!"

Zelpha dropped fast, her hands above her head a cry torn from her mouth.

Hildy also started to let go just as a sudden strong updraft caught the massive dirigible, sending it shooting upward so fast it took Hildy's breath away. She instinctively clamped both hands tighter about the cable and held on, aware that Spud was doing the same.

Hildy glanced down and gasped. The earth seemed to fall away, faster and faster. She and Spud dangled helplessly from the cable until they were about a hundred feet in the air.

Hildy closed her eyes against the horrible sight. Her silent prayer was like a scream of fright.

O Lord, No!

CHAPTER
TWENTY-ONE

STARK TERROR

Saturday

The wind shrieked in Hildy's face and whipped the heavy metal cable around like a string in a tornado. With her eyes closed, Hildy desperately tightened her hands about the landing line. At the same time, she was aware that the end dangled about six feet below her aching hands. She tried wrapping her legs around the line, but the wind whipped it away from her body.

Her weight seemed about to wrench her arms from their sockets. She moaned in agony and fear.

Spud yelled in her ear, "Hang on!"

The wind tore the boy's words away so they were barely audible, even from inches away. Hildy nodded. She opened her eyes.

"Don't look down!" Spud shouted. "They'll get it under control in a moment!"

Stark terror and the wind in her face sucked Hildy's breath away so she could not answer. She managed to nod wordlessly while forcing her eyes to stay open against the cutting wind. She didn't mean to ignore Spud's words, but the fascination was too great. She glanced down.

In that instant, a photographic image was burned into Hildy's memory.

The dirigible's hangar, nearly twelve-hundred feet long, lay off to her right. The great open end was so wide a football field could have been slid in lengthwise with room to spare. Behind the hangar, taller than a twenty-story building, there were row upon row of workers' cars in the parking lot.

Buses lined up like railroad cars along the main road appeared to be no bigger than children's toys. The bleachers were almost directly below. The spectators looked up, mouths open in disbelief. In front of the front row and off to one side, two newsreel cameras were pointed up. Hildy could see the cameramen, their caps turned around backward, eyes pressed to their instruments, recording the incredible event taking place.

The vast open landing field stretched just beyond the newsreel cameramen. The field was empty except for the two-hundred-foot mooring mast and scattered blue-clad sailors in white caps. Their heads were tipped back, their eyes focused on the giant airship and the hapless victims swinging from landing cables far above.

Hildy fought the wind, which forced itself down her open mouth so she could barely breathe. She turned to look at Spud's face. Instead of his usual ruddy color, he was so pale that his freckles stood out sharply.

Hildy managed to gasp, "My hands—are getting numb!"

"Don't think about it. Just think about holding on! It won't be much longer. Look up! See? I think we're slowing a little." Spud's words were shredded by the wind, but they were a little clearer than before.

Hildy nodded and willed herself to look up. She was startled to see several sailors hanging on to other cables along the entire length of the airship. She shuddered, remembering the homeroom report about a newsreel in which line handlers trying to moor a dirigible had fallen to their deaths.

O Lord! The silent prayer was powerfully earnest. *Please help us all to hang on!*

Hildy's hands were dead lumps with only a faint sensation

of skinned palms, but her shoulders ached with such excruciating pain that she wanted to scream. Hildy fought down that impulse as her view slid up from the hapless sailors. Off to the west, she glimpsed the peaceful blue Pacific Ocean.

Then she looked straight up. The dirigible's size was awesome. It seemed to stretch forever in both directions, casting a dark shadow that engulfed her and Spud. On the underside and slightly up from the bottom of the great ship, motors hummed with the distinctive sound peculiar to dirigibles. Silvery propellers whirled in the bright sun.

Slowly the scenes around her seemed to grow dim. She felt less and less pain in her shoulders, hands, and arms. *I wonder if this means I'm dying?*

For a second, Hildy was tempted to yield to the easy choice of letting go and falling. Then a thought flickered through her mind. *This one thing I do . . .*

Hildy felt a surge of hope. *I can't die! Not now! That'd be the end of everything—the scholarship, family, friends—the end of our 'forever' home . . .*

"Don't give up!" Spud's shout in her ears broke Hildy's thoughts.

Hildy nodded, wanting to say, *I won't!* but she could feel herself getting weaker. Her hands started to slip.

Spud exclaimed, "Listen!"

Hildy heard a new sound, like wind moaning in the top of pine trees. But there was no wind, and now she could breathe without having her breath taken away.

Hildy asked weakly, "What is it? Sounds almost—human."

"It *is* human! Look!"

Hildy glanced down. A massive sea of faces stared up with open mouths. Continuous gasps and cries poured from the crowd.

Then Hildy blinked and looked again, because their faces seemed to be rushing upward. Realization of what was happening hit her. "We're coming down!"

Spud warned, "Don't let go until we touch down!"

Hildy nodded, wearily watching as the line handlers on the

ground swarmed toward the dangling cables. A mighty roar of hope and triumph tore from the throats of the spectators as the sailors began to tug and the huge airship slowly eased under ground control.

Hildy felt arms encircle her body. A white-capped sailor in blue uniform had his face inches from her. "You can let go now—both of you! You're safe!"

Hildy felt the solid ground under her feet. She looked at Spud and tried to smile. She thought he tried to smile back, but she wasn't sure. Her hands slipped off the landing line, and she sank into her rescuer's arms.

———

It was late that afternoon before Hildy finally was finished with the official military questions, the precautionary physical examinations, and posing self-consciously with Spud for the insistent newsreel cameramen and the swarming newspaper reporters. But at last it was over, and Hildy happily allowed Ben to lead her and Spud away to the old Ranger's Packard.

They had barely reached the parking lot when Hildy heard her name called. She groaned inwardly, not wanting to answer one more question. She kept walking, but the call was persistent and coming closer. Hildy sighed and turned around, then blinked in surprise.

Zelpha stopped and stood awkwardly for a moment, her mouth moving but with no words emerging. Hildy didn't know what to say, so she waited in silence.

"Hildy," Zelpha finally said, "I—uh, thanks for what you did for me back there." She motioned toward where the dirigible was securely moored. "You, too, Spud."

Hildy and Spud nodded. Hildy said, "I'm glad you're okay, Zelpha."

"I did a foolish thing," she continued, "trying to make my father notice me. He's never going to change, I guess, even after what just happened. He told me a few minutes ago there's a recall movement going on to force him off the school board.

"Anyway, Hildy I—I'm sorry about the things I said and the

way I treated you. I'll never again call anyone an Okie. I'm also sorry about writing the note and then stealing it. I told Aunt Poppy about it just now. She knows you were unfairly blamed."

"Thank you, Zelpha."

"Your father was right about it not mattering where a person is born or where he comes from. It's what you become or where you're going that counts. I know that now. I live in a big house and have lots of nice things, but I'd trade them for what you've got. As for the essay, I know that you're going to win the contest, and the scholarship, and I'm glad. I really am."

Hildy reached out and put her arms around Zelpha. "I'm glad we can be friends."

After church the next day, Mr. and Mrs. Farnham hosted a reception for everyone involved in the rescue of their daughter. The banker rose from his position at the far end of the long table and asked Ben to return thanks. As he did so, Hildy was filled with gratitude, and she had her own silent prayer thoughts.

Thanks for answering my prayers! They helped strengthen my faith. Thanks for those who sit around this table in safety and love after some scary times. Thanks, too, that all of us survived the dirigible experience. I can write about that in my essay. Thanks that faith in Thy plans helped me to hang on up there. May I never lose sight of the vision Thou hast given me for my life, and never stop pressing on toward the mark.

Hildy opened her eyes at Ben's "Amen," which was echoed around the table.

The banker stood and cleared his throat. "Before we begin eating, my wife and I would like to announce that a trust fund has been set up at the bank for Hildy, Spud, and Ruby for their dramatic rescue of our kidnapped daughter. It will guarantee higher education or a start in adult life for three incredible young people!"

Hildy looked with wide, startled eyes at Ruby and Spud.

Mr. Farnham continued, "My wife and I hope that we can become Spud's guardian so he can enter school and live where people love him. But for now, let's rejoice in all that's good." He turned to look at his daughter. "Connie, I'm so glad you're . . ."

His voice broke, and he couldn't finish. He sat down with tears in his eyes.

Hildy leaned over and hugged the little girl, then smiled happily at everyone around the table. Tomorrow would bring new problems, like moving and continuing to survive in these hard times, but Hildy was ready. She knew her goal, and she was eager to continue reaching toward it.

DISCARD

CHEMEKETA COOPERATIVE REGIONAL LIBRARY SERVICE

3 3610 02811 0846

12-03

Sf

Lyons Public Library
44
P.O. Box 100
DISCARD
Lyons, OR 97358